A LETTER TO
THE PRESIDENT OF
THE UNITED STATES . . .

Dear Mr. President:

It has become a common, but erroneous, American dictum that an offense always overwhelms a defense. Yet Stalingrad and the Battle of Britain, to name two examples within memory, proved that a good defense can defeat a vigorous offense. We believe that a stable peace is best assured by a balance of offense and defense; and that *even a modestly effective defense* can powerfully deter a first strike by any aggressor.

We believe that several systems, both kinetic and directed energy systems, should be developed concurrently for a spectrum of strategic defenses. After years of neglect of strategic defense, we find it imperative that several avenues be pursued concurrently. We must not have a triad of offense and a monad of defense.

While we agree that point defenses by kinetic energy weapons serve an immediate need and should be developed, we believe the nation should vigorously investigate the uses of space for strategic defense.

We believe it is imperative that we first address four candidate systems which provide a significant military capability, i.e., to deny assurance of first-strike success by any aggressor by 1990.

• Multiple satellite using kinetic energy kill.
• Ground-based lasers and mirrors in space.
• Space-based lasers.
• Nuclear explosive-driven beam technologies collectively known as third generation systems.
• Ground based point defense systems.

We also urge greatly-accelerated research on the many other candidate systems, including particle-beam weapons, which offer promise on the longer term.

Implicit in the adoption of our recommendations are the requirements to state openly and unequivocally our intent to adopt a balanced offensive-defensive national strategy and to assess the spectrum of threats and technical risks associated with actual deployment.

Systems Assessment Group

Citizens Advisory Council on National Space Policy

Daniel O. Graham, Lt. Gen. USA (Ret.)
Maxwell Hunter, Ph.D.
Francis X. Kane, Ph.D., Col. USAF (Ret.)
Stewart Meyer, Maj. Gen. USA (Ret.)
Dennis A. Reilly, Ph.D
Lowell W. Wood, Ph.D.

The report of the Systems Assessment Group has received the unanimous approval of the Council.

J. E. Pournelle, Ph.D.
Chairman

MUTUAL ASSURED SURVIVAL

Jerry E. Pournelle, Ph.D., F.A.R.S.
Dean Ing, Ph.D.

The Citizens Advisory Council on National Space Policy is sponsored by The L-5 Society Promoting Space Development. Responsibility for arguments and conclusions of the Council rests with the Council Members and individual authors.

The Council gratefully acknowledges the support of the L-5 Society and The Vaughn Foundation.

This work is based on the Report to the President of the Citizens Advisory Council on National Space Policy. The full report, including all technical appendices, is available from the L-5 Society, 1060 E. Elm St., Tucson, AZ 85719, for a donation of $7.50 to the Society. The L-5 Society invites membership applications; annual dues are $25.00 ($15.00 student membership).

A BAEN BOOK

A Baen Book

Baen Enterprises
8-10 W. 36th Street
New York, N.Y. 10018

First printing, November 1984.

ISBN: 0-671-55923-0

Cover art by Larry Selman.

Printed in the United States of America

Distributed by
SIMON & SCHUSTER
MASS MERCHANDISE SALES COMPANY
1230 Avenue of the Americas
New York, N.Y. 10020

MUTUAL ASSURED SURVIVAL

Jerry E. Pournelle, Ph.D., F.A.R.S.
Dean Ing, Ph.D.

This book is dedicated to
Mrs. Marilyn Niven

CONTENTS

CITIZENS ADVISORY COUNCIL ON NATIONAL SPACE POLICY

SUMMER 1983 MEETING

MEMBERSHIP

Buzz Aldrin, D.Sc., Col. USAF (Ret.), Former Astronaut
James Patrick Baen, Editor and Publisher
Greg Bear, Writer
Gregory Benford, Ph.D., Professor of Physics
James Benford, Ph.D., Nuclear Physicist
Robert Bussard, Ph.D., Nuclear Physicist
Philip Chapman, Ph.D., Former Astronaut.
Michael Gamble, Aerospace Engineer
Joseph Goodwin, Aerospace Engineer
Daniel O. Graham, Lt. Gen. USA, (Ret.)
Fred Haise, Former Astronaut
Robert A. Heinlein, Writer
Mark Hopkins, Economist
Gary Hudson, Space Systems Consultant
Maxwell Hunter, Ph.D., Aerospace Scientist
Rod Hyde, Ph.D., High Energy Physicist
Michael Hyson, Ph.D., Biophysicist
Dean Ing, Ph.D., Writer
Francis X. Kane, Ph.D., Col. USAF (Ret.)
Arthur Kantrowitz, Ph.D., N.A.S., Development
  Scientist
Arnold Kramish, Ph.D., Physicist
John McCarthy, Ph.D., Professor of Computer Science
George Merrick, Aerospace Engineer
Stewart Meyer, Maj. Gen. USA (Ret.)
Colin Mick, Ph.D., Computer Scientist
Marvin Minsky, Ph.D., Professor of Computer Science
Larry Niven, Writer
Stefan T. Possony, Ph.D., Intelligence Specialist
Alexander Pournelle, Student
J. E. Pournelle, Ph.D., Writer
James Ransom, Aerospace Engineer
Dennis Reilly, Ph.D., High Energy Physicist

Membership (*continued*)

Jennifer Roth, Student
Robert Salkeld, Systems Propulsion Specialist
Horst Salzwedel, Ph.D., Computer Consultant
G. Harry Stine, Writer
Bjo Trimble, Homemaker
J. Peter Vajk, Ph.D., Physicist
James Miller Vaughn, Jr., Foundation Executive
Lowell Wood, Ph.D., Nuclear Physicist
Gordon Woodcock, Aerospace Engineer

The Citizens Advisory Council on National Space Policy is sponsored by The L-5 Society Promoting Space Development. Responsibility for arguments and conclusions of the Council rests with the Council Members and individual authors.

The Council gratefully acknowledges the support of the L-5 Society and The Vaughn Foundation.

PREFACE

New Hope for a Frightened World

"There has been a great deal said about a 3,000-mile high-angle rocket ... I don't think anyone in the world knows how to do such a thing, and I feel confident that it will not be done for a long period of time to come ... I think we can leave that out of our thinking. I wish the American public would leave that out of their thinking."
—**Dr. Vannevar Bush, Testimony to Congress, 1945.**

"The only defense against the weapons of the future is to prevent them ever being used. In other words, the problem is political and not military at all. A country's armed forces can no longer defend it; the most they can promise is the destruction of the attacker...."
—**Arthur C. Clarke, "The Rocket and the Future of Warfare," 1946.**

13

"O thus be it ever, when free men shall stand, between their loved homes, and the war's desolation . . ."
—**Francis Scott Key,** *The Star Spangled Banner.*

"No price is too high if we can make these terrible weapons obsolete and irrelevant."
—**George Brown, Member of Congress (Democrat, California) at the L-5 Society Annual Space Development Conference, 1984.**

Earth is well-armed. There are about 20,000 nuclear weapons, some unimaginably powerful and each with at least the destructive power of the Hiroshima Bomb, poised and waiting for someone to push the button. Every year, more nuclear weapons are added to the strategic inventory.

For over thirty years the offensive power of the nuclear-tipped Intercontinental Ballistic Missile has dominated military planning and nearly paralyzed strategic thought. Whole generations have grown up in the shadow of nuclear terror, as East and West accumulate ever more bombs and missiles. There seems no help for this: the only way to preserve freedom has been to live in the shadow of death by preserving the balance of terror.

On March 23, 1983, the President of the United States proposed a challenge to American scientists and engineers. Could they, as the fifth decade of the Atomic Age nears, dismantle the balance of terror while preserving freedom? Could American science, technology, and industry do what the diplomats have failed to achieve?

Responses varied. The President spoke after taking the considered advice of more than a score of the top scientists and engineers in the nation; but within minutes, a number of Members of Congress went before the nation to ridicule the President as "Darth Vader" and to label his proposal to end our nuclear nightmare "Star Wars." Within hours they were joined

by a great chorus of intellectuals who seemed over-
joyed to point out that there is no defense against
the ICBM; assured survival is not possible, and rather
than develop a strategy of Mutual Assured Survival,
we must rely on the strategy of Mutual Assured
Destruction.

Others thought President Reagan's proposed Strategic Defense Initiative a bright ray of hope in a
world weary of the threat of annihilation. Could it
be possible that the long dominance of offensive
power might be brought to an end, and a new era of
defense begun? Soldier and civilian alike can rejoice
if it is once again possible for free men—and women—
to stand between their loved homes and the war's
desolation. Surely it must be worth trying.

In the summer of 1983, a remarkable group of
scientists and other citizens met in Tarzana, California to examine new options in strategy. Democrats and
Republicans, conservatives and liberals, physicists,
engineers, writers, students, and housewives, they
were united by two aims. First, they were all familiar with new developments in space and technology,
and enthusiastically believed that mankind can and
must expand into space. Second, they wished to take
a hard look at the possibilities of new science and
technology for the defense of the west; to see whether,
in the President's words, we now have the opportunity to make the ICBM "obsolete and irrelevant."

This book tells what happened at that meeting.
The news is good.

Jerry E. Pournelle, Hollywood, 1984
Dean Ing, Ashland, Oregon, 1984

A Report to the
President of the United States

Late in July of 1983, the Citizens Advisory Council on National Space Policy convened at the Tarzana, California home of Mr. and Mrs. Lawrence Van Cott Niven. This would be their third meeting.

The Council was formed in 1980 by the joint actions of Dr. Charles Sheffield, then the President of the American Astronautical Society, and Gerald Driggers, at that time President of the L-5 Society Promoting Space Development. After the initial meeting, the Council continued under the sponsorship of the L-5 Society, although its reports are the sole responsibility of the Council membership. The third meeting of the Council was devoted to defense. Surprisingly, the results of that meeting were unanimous; not only did each of those who attended agree to the final report, but a number of others, unable to attend, signed it after reading the final draft.

This Executive Summary Report was submitted to the President of the United States on 28 September, 1983.

EXECUTIVE SUMMARY REPORT

SPACE AND ASSURED SURVIVAL

CONCLUSIONS AND RECOMMENDATIONS OF THE
REPORT TO THE PRESIDENT OF THE
CITIZENS ADVISORY COUNCIL

CONCLUSIONS

1. **The President's proposal to change the defensive posture of the United States from Mutual Assured Destruction to Assured Survival is morally correct, technologically feasible, and economically desirable.** The United States faces threats which cannot easily be countered by continued reliance on MAD. Immediate action is required to assure our national security.
2. **Significant improvements to national security can be made before the end of this decade.** To achieve this, we must begin immediate deployment of defensive systems, as well as greatly increase our research and development efforts.
   Defense of the United States will require a variety of mutually supporting systems. No system is perfect. However, we cannot afford to wait. We must begin deployment **now.**
3. **Defense of the nation will require direct Presidential action and support.** We have both the technical

knowledge and the industrial capability to deploy effective defenses. However, it will not be done in time with existing management structures and bureaucratic organizations. A new program office, reporting directly to the Secretary of Defense, and organized like the Manhattan Project, will be required.

*   *   *

RECOMMENDATIONS

1. We recommend immediate funding to develop and deploy a wide range of defensive systems and technologies. These must include:

- Multiple satellites using kinetic energy kill.
- Ground-based lasers with mirrors in space.
- Space-based laser systems.
- Nuclear-explosive driven beam technologies, collectively known as third generation systems.
- Ground-based point defense systems.

We also urge greatly accelerated research on the many other candidate systems, such as particle beam weapons, which offer promise on the longer term.

2. We recommend immediate **deployment** of these systems, as well as the development of required transportation systems for space-based systems.

3. We recommend that deployment of these systems be entrusted to a special unified management organization headed by a program director reporting directly to the Secretary of Defense. This appointment should be made as soon as possible.

Certain of the individual and committee papers that accompanied the Executive Summary Report were such models of concision and advocacy that they could hardly be improved; the authors have elected to incorporate some of them virtually unchanged as appendices to Mutual Assured Survival.

CHAPTER ONE

An Old Bankruptcy,
A New Currency

The so-called "Missile Gap" was a decisive factor in the election of 1960. Now we know that it was illusory; the Soviet Union not only did not have a lead in strategic missiles, but in fact had no real missile capability whatever. After the Cuban missile crisis of 1962 was resolved in U.S. favor largely because of U.S. strategic missile superiority, the Soviets determined never again to allow that to happen. From the early 1960's on they concentrated on developing a commanding lead in intercontinental strategic nuclear power.

By 1970 they had installed four different ICBM assembly lines, and by 1972 these were running three shifts, twenty-four hours a day. Today, in 1984, they continue to operate full time.

By 1978 (and possibly before) the Soviets had achieved strategic superiority, at least in numbers of missiles and deliverable warheads. Superiority is a problematical thing in the nuclear era. There is no point in having an overwhelming capability for destruction if your own nation will also be destroyed.

Translating strategic superiority into international political advantage is no simple matter—until you achieve overwhelming superiority, enough to destroy the opponent's ability to strike back.

For a number of years strategists considered a "clean win" to be impossible. Hawks and doves could agree: the best way, the only way, to survive a nuclear war is not to have one.

This is still true, but the situation is changing. As technology develops there could come a time when one side can destroy the other's strategic nuclear forces so thoroughly that no retaliation would be possible. If the Soviet Union ever achieves such superiority, their past actions indicate they will try to translate that capability into strategic power. That will not be a stable world.

The debate over national strategic doctrine has profound implications for the future of the human race. George Orwell said, "If you want a picture of the future, imagine a boot stamping on a human face—forever." If we are to avoid that fate; if we are to preserve freedom and Western Civilization in an era in which the Soviet Union has strategic superiority, we must use every possible advantage. This includes properly exploiting our technologies, and developing superior strategies.

This is difficult but not impossible. The United States holds numerous advantages. We must develop strategies to take advantage of them.

The Origin of MAD

During the Eisenhower Administration, the official doctrine of the United States was "massive retaliation". President Eisenhower defined this as a determination to meet any attack on the U.S. or our allies "with massive retaliation at a time and place of our own choosing." At that time we had the strategic power to make good such a threat.

Shortly after taking office in 1961, Secretary of Defense Robert S. McNamara attended a briefing by the Commander-in-Chief of the Strategic Air Command (SAC). The general showed the Secretary the SIOP—the Single Integrated Operational Plan which would control U.S. strategic weapons in the event of all-out war with the Soviet Union. The SIOP consisted of a target list based on the best intelligence information available to SAC, and a schedule for the elimination of those targets. Every weapon in the U.S. inventory was allocated, and all would be launched within 36 hours.

When the briefing was completed, McNamara expressed horror. "General," he said, "you don't have a war plan. All you have is a kind of horrible spasm."

McNamara was determined to reform the U.S. strategic doctrines, and to give the President a series of options. The new policy was to be called "Flexible Response." Soon, however, McNamara found that "flexible response" would require great skill, sophisticated new weapons, and a lot of money which would have to be extracted from Johnson's "Great Society." While the Congress might then have been willing to pay the price, Johnson and McNamara were not. In part on the advice of a new school of "civilian strategists" trained mostly in Eastern university schools of social science, McNamara opted for a new doctrine.

This was called "Assured Destruction" and was based on the hostage theory. If both the U.S. and Soviet populations would inevitably be destroyed in any nuclear war, then that war would never happen. The United States need not try to retain strategic superiority, because superiority was impossible. "Sufficiency" would be enough. Moreover, the Soviets would soon come to agree. According to the new theory, the only reason the Soviet Union built strategic weapons was from fear of the U.S. weapons; if we stopped building nuclear-tipped ICBMs, so would the Soviets. Given sufficiency on both sides, we would have a highly stable world; a world of Mutual Assured Destruction, or MAD.

This theory was made the basis of U.S. doctrine: after we deployed 1000 Minuteman missiles, we built no more. The Soviets would now be given a chance to catch up, after which we would negotiate an arms control agreement to stabilize the situation.

They caught up.

They passed us.

They continued to install new missiles. They ringed Europe with their mobile SS-20 missiles, and while developing the capability to reload their existing strategic silos to allow multiple salvoes. Note that this capability can *only* be used for first strikes, since the "reload" missiles are very vulnerable.

To this day they halt not, neither do they slow: their four production lines continue to turn out new nuclear-armed ICBMs 24 hours a day. They have achieved strategic superiority; we must now live with that.

After the election of 1980, President-elect Ronald Reagan asked a number of private citizen groups to provide briefing papers for the new administration. Some of those groups continued after the inauguration. One such group was the Citizens Advisory Council on National Space Policy. Originally sponsored by the Presidents of the American Astronautical Society and the L-5 Society, the Council is largely made up of experts in space science and engineering; but it also includes enthusiasts, home makers, writers, students, and other interested citizens.

The Council is interested in space policy. All members of the Council have agreed that without a rational U.S. defense policy, there can be no U.S. space program. Although all the Council members believe in the defense of the United States, there were considerable disagreements about the nature and feasibility of defensive weapons systems. Many scientists and technologists did not believe defense was possible at all.

The Council was therefore expanded to include several of the nation's foremost experts in laser systems, as well as military planners, computer scientists, and nuclear physicists. The third meeting of the Council was devoted to investigating defense feasibilities and reconciling differences among experts. The goal was to produce a detailed report on defense of the U.S. After long discussion, a report that every member could adopt was drafted. The Council Report, available in its original form from the L-5 Society, was read by the President, and received a letter of commendation from him.

This book is based on that report.

* * *

The Citizens Advisory Council is nearly unique in that it includes not only some of the top scientific and technical talent in the nation, but also a number of technically oriented science fiction writers. Their value is highlighted by the results of a recent national news service poll. Of more than a dozen categories of "noted Americans" ranging from chief executives of Fortune 500 companies to politicians, only science fiction writers perceived the *political* importance of space research. The writer members of the Council could hardly fail to see this importance, because most of them were initially trained as physicists and engineers.

Throughout that long July weekend, while discussions spilled out of the spacious Niven home into the warmth of the California evening, members traded good-natured political jokes along with information and expert insights. Several members remarked on their heightened awareness that the goal of the Council transcended ordinary political labels. A conservative could rebel against a policy that maximizes threats against innocent Russian children, yet remain conservative. A liberal could recognize the crucial importance of a *defensive* presence in space, and still be a liberal.

Many of the Council members had special views to impart—a favorite system of hardware, or a particular set of priorities toward the national good. Some of these views were bound to meet head-to-head in committee sessions, and those sessions were always lively (occasionally acrimonious). But narrow vested interests were always subordinated to the single, overriding vested interest of the Council: to outline a specific and complete alternative to this nation's declared nuclear strategy of Mutually Assured Destruction (MAD).

The original arguments for MAD could have had some validity when then-Secretary of Defense Robert McNamara espoused them in the 1960s. They could have, that is, if the Soviet Union had accepted them. MAD always depended on the *mutual* belief that whichever of the superpowers initiated a nuclear war, both nations would be utterly annihilated: Mutual Assured Destruction. Mutual MADness, if you will.

Now, a generation later, we see overwhelming evidence that the Soviets do not now and never did believe in MAD. They have, however, profited enormously from *our* belief in it. We dismantled our fledgling antiballistic missile (ABM) system and we largely abandoned our Civil Defense plans which might (still!) save a hundred million American lives. We openly admitted that our cities were hostage to the Soviets. To this moment we are hostages still.

As for the Soviet strategy: they have an upgraded ABM system protecting Moscow, and they have a vigorous, continuing C D establishment which directly involves over twenty *million* Soviet citizens trained as a nuclear survival cadre. In addition, they have tested advanced antisatellite weapon systems that might make us incapable of responding to a nuclear first strike. In short, the Soviet Union clearly plans to survive nuclear war. This isn't to suggest that Soviet planners envision a holocaust without damage to themselves, nor that they necessarily plan to start such a war. It *does* show that, unlike us, they do not despair of surviving that war; if it comes, they intend to win it. That, they proclaim and believe, is the very purpose of governments.

Since MAD always depended on both sides believing in it, our MAD strategy has not bought us a stable, peaceful future. It cannot even purchase parity in weaponry when our opponent is developing offensive orbital weapons. MAD is not merely threadbare; it is bankrupt.

This conclusion was the cement binding Council members toward a common goal. The U.S. doesn't need more nuclear warheads with more terrifying offensive capability. Nor can we match the Soviets in their huge conventional armaments without severe economic problems. Instead, we need an alternative to MAD; a less provocatively offensive, more prudently defensive strategy. For maximum effectiveness, the new strategy must be based on our strengths and its validity must *not* fundamentally depend upon unverifiable and unenforceable agreements. Finally, an optimum U.S. strategy will provide hope for a future that escapes the gloomy prediction of groups like the Club of Rome and their well-known report, *The Limits To Growth*. It's not enough that we abandon the bankruptcy of MAD; we must generate a vital new currency.

Even in the 1950s a few far-sighted strategic theorists understood that the Intercontinental Ballistic Missile (ICBM) was not necessarily an ultimate weapon, and that alternatives to MAD were possible. Some were military officers who understood that MAD was not truly mutual, because the Soviet Union would never accept the doctrine. They argued persuasively for their views; but true to their oaths, when decisions were made by civilian political authorities, they obeyed orders.

Others were civilians: strategists, scientists, engineers, systems analysts in the aerospace industry, who had been involved in long range planning studies. Their research showed new technologies not yet available, but which when they came on line would negate the power of the ICBM. These far-sighted planners urged development of these systems, including ways to intercept missiles in flight. All of the best strategists, military and civilian, understood that the ICBM was no "ultimate weapon," that indeed there can be no ultimate weapons. It is the nature of the technological war that there are no final answers. Every new development has within it the seeds of a counter weapon. The technological war will never end. Fortunately, the battles in that war are generally bloodless.

By the 1960s both the U.S. and the Soviets had proof that an ICBM could be intercepted. The United States worked from theoretical analysis of weapons effects. The Soviets moved rapidly to actual tests. In one test they launched three ICBM re-entry vehicles (RV's) and detonated a nuclear interception weapon near the first. This gave them considerable data on the effects of nuclear weapons in space and the upper atmosphere. Before the United States could repeat those tests, the Soviets agreed to an atmospheric Test Ban Treaty. This gave the Soviets a considerable lead in ICBM defense technology.

In 1964 the Soviets paraded their newest ICBM interceptor, which NATO gave the code name "GALOSH". This interceptor missile used a nuclear warhead designed to detonate above the atmosphere. The presumed kill mechanism was a surge of hard X-rays which would disrupt an incoming RV and its nuclear warhead.

The U.S. system was designated "SAFEGUARD" and employed both the Spartan, which was designed for very high altitude intercept much like the Soviet Galosh, and the Sprint. Both employed nuclear warheads; the Sprint used a comparatively low yield weapon. The Sprint, a two-stage solid propelled rocket, boasted an acceleration so high that, two seconds after launch, it was a mile above the launcher. Of course the Sprint was intended to intercept its target much higher (its range was twenty-five miles). But by this time we had discovered some of the subtler effects of a nuclear detonation. We had seen how a nuclear airburst could generate an electromagnetic pulse (EMP) that could devastate communication and computer equipment thousands of miles away. U.S. nuclear warheads detonated over our own soil, even many miles high above our soil, were, to put it mildly, not an attractive proposition. Many on this Council would argue that even the most devastating EMP pulse would be cheap compared to a groundburst, but that is an issue for another book.

Some designers pointed out that ballistic missile warheads travel at such enormous speeds (several miles per second) that they could be destroyed by "kinetic energy kill," meaning impact with a hunk of material no larger than a bullet, or even a small stone. If we could hurl a device into the path of an incoming warhead and then distribute tiny pieces of material, shotgun style, so that the warhead could not avoid them all, we would destroy that warhead. This kinetic energy kill scheme was relatively simple, it was non-nuclear, and particles that missed their targets would burn up harmlessly, high above our soil.

Other kill mechanisms, including directed nuclear debris, were also possible. In a series of papers published in 1968, and later in their book *The Strategy of Technology*, Stefan T. Possony and Jerry E. Pournelle argued that the United States should abandon the doctrine of Assured Destruction, and instead adopt a strategy of Assured Survival. Specific proposals included conversion of a portion of the existing Minuteman missiles to defensive systems, together with deployment of sufficient offensive Minuteman systems to bring the force back to strength.

Defensive systems included both "pop-up" area protection missiles designed to foil a massive Soviet strike, and hardened command, communications, control, and intelligence (C^3I) systems to allow damage assessment and precision employment of the surviving Minuteman force.

The debate over U.S. grand strategy—Assured Destruction vs. Assured Survival—was carried out at high levels in the government, but never became part of public or Congressional debate. Most of the arguments were technical. Many engineers and scientists doubted our ability to detect and track intercontinental missiles. There were more misgivings about the ability to place an interceptor missile precisely in the path of an incoming warhead. Although many highly qualified members of the technical community were convinced that the United States would be able to develop reliable non-nuclear kill mechanisms sufficient to protect the Titan and Minuteman bases, the conventional wisdom of the time was that "we cannot hit a bullet with a bullet."

Instead, the MAD strategy was adopted. The iron logic of MAD required that all defensive systems, including civil defense, be abandoned. The original plans for the Interstate Highway System included fallout and blast shelters to be constructed within many of the freeway on-ramps. This plan had already suffered under McNamara and Johnson; it was now abandoned. Meanwhile, negotiators were sent to procure by Arms Control agreements the security the United States refused to provide itself through technology.

Under the terms of the Ballistic Missile Defense Treaty (separate from, but signed on the same day as the Strategic Arms Limitation Treaty or SALT), the U.S. and the Soviet Union could each retain one Anti-Ballistic Missile (ABM) system. For a short period of time we experimented with such a system to protect the missile bases in Montana. The Soviets chose to protect missile sites in the suburbs of Moscow.

The Soviet Union has recently begun to expand their Moscow ABM system, and are now upgrading it with hypervelocity Sprint-type rockets. They have also deployed long range radar arrays suitable for nuclear battle-management far from their borders, in clear violation of the ABM Treaty. Our only ABM system was dismantled nearly a decade ago.

Two arguments were given for discarding ABM. First, the most influential technical analysts discarded the concept of non-nuclear interception as infeasible, not recognizing that research and development would soon produce new means (such as on-board micro computers) for greatly increasing intercept accuracy.

Secondly, it was argued, defensive systems are illogical, since the doctrine of MAD demands that both sides remain perfectly vulnerable. If both U.S. and Soviet populations are hostage, then peace is assured; and anything which mitigates the horrors of war paradoxically increases the chances that war will begin. The Soviets have never accepted this argument.

Moreover, when lasers were first developed, a number of laser scientists argued that lasers would never be powerful enough to destroy or damage aircraft and missiles. Certainly early laser systems were insufficient; the early lasers were both low power and inefficient. However, a decade later, the United States openly demonstrated an airborne antimissile laser that can and does destroy not only aircraft, but also small air-to-air missiles in flight. Beam technologies are still in their infancy, and even more dramatic advances can be expected.

During the 1970s, advances in semiconductors, infrared sensors, and radar provided very much better target acquisition. It began to look as if impact weapons might indeed be able to stop a bullet with a bullet. But it looked that way only to a few who bothered to plug in the new advances, and to consider some fresh conclusions. By the mid-1970s, those few were already working to convince others that MAD was fatally flawed; not only was it now feasible to defend against ICBMs, but the Soviets appeared to be working feverishly toward that very goal. Indeed, in some of the most promising areas of research the Soviets were ahead of us even then. During the late 1970s, some Council members were arguing that MAD was obsolete, and that with its new technologies the U.S. could devise strategic defense worthy of the name. Such a system would at worst save many millions of lives by protecting our population and, by its very presence, lessen the attractiveness of a first strike.

The deterrence of a defense system that is only somewhat effective is absurdly underrated by critics.

Professor William Baugh (both a physicist and political scientist) has explained it succinctly in his even-
handed new textbook, *The Politics of Nuclear Balance.*
As Baugh puts it, "The intent in building such a
defense is not to achieve perfection in the form of
zero enemy penetration, but to reduce enemy penetration to the point that any attack is deterred by
uncertainty about its effects." In other words, if your
enemy's missile farms might survive it, the attractiveness of a first strike is much reduced.

By mid-1983, Council members had already shown
that such strategies could be developed. A few of
their reports are reprinted verbatim here. But could
the heartfelt views of thirty experts be abraded down
to something approaching a unanimous opinion without erasing all detail in the process? A man who has
spent thirty years cursing experimental devices that
determinedly resist translation into foolproof, mass-
producible hardware has a natural inbred reluctance
to bet on an unproved technology—just as a scientist
who has seen his experimental hardware perform
several orders of magnitude better than older gadgetry,
is unlikely to opt for yesterday's systems.

It was Jerry Pournelle who kept the various committees, deliberating in separated portions of chez
Niven, aware of developments elsewhere in the house.
Sometimes a committee member would be invited
by the Chairman to take a half-hour sabbatical with
another group. Almost as often the roving Chairman,
upon finding that a committee had reached consensus on some detail, passed the datum on to the other
committees. There are times when the timbre and
decibel level of Chairman Pournelle's voice are sorely
needed; the July Council meeting was one of those
times. In this way, the various groups managed to
avoid the false starts and reiterations that plague so
many large councils.

The findings of the Systems Assessment Group were
particularly crucial for several reasons. Its members
included top-ranked experts in several areas of defense technology (although the discussions remained

on an unclassified level); and it was their task to decide which systems proposed by the other groups would be most effective in defending against nuclear attack.

For an example, some defensive weaponry would not require a continuing human presence in space. Those that did might require manned space stations, a longer development time, or a lunar settlement. Clearly, the report of the Systems Assessment Group would figure in the deliberations of the committees on strategy and economics. But information flowed in all directions; there was no advantage in recommending a system which had inferior strategic value, or which was inordinately expensive even if it did fry the proposer's fish particularly well.

On the evening of Saturday, 30 July 1983, the Systems Assessment Group drafted a set of recommendations that was read in plenary session. The other committees, already provided with "leaks" as to the general nature of those recommendations, were also ready with portions of a letter to the White House stating the findings of the Council. That letter forms part of the introduction to this volume. The President's gracious response is photo-reproduced on the back cover of this volume and as an end paper.

Inevitably, the plenary session unearthed minor disagreements which required resolution. It was the intent of the Chairman to extract, somehow, a letter draft that was unanimously acceptable to attending members. Perfect unanimity still escaped us at the end of the Saturday session, but by then we were all satisfied with the content of the letter. The only remaining problems lay with the phrasing. One engineer, easing into the Niven Jacuzzi that night, wryly voiced a consensus opinion: "We don't have many writers," he grinned, "but every s.o.b. with a pencil thinks he's an editor. . . ."

On Sunday, 31 July 1983, another plenary session yielded phrasing that was acceptable to every member present. Since the letter emanated from the Systems Assessment Group, it was quite brief, addressing only the imperative of specific defenses against ballistic missiles. MAD was not even mentioned; it was simply superseded by implication. Other Council recommendations were collated for inclusion in a 135-page summary report, which was submitted to the White House later. The essence of those findings are the heart of this book. They range from the industrial exploitation of space to the strategic question of stability and our belief that the Soviets and others should be invited to develop space-based ballistic missile defenses of their own. Also, the findings provided a data base for subsequent meetings of the Council. They gave us reason for optimism, not only for citizens under the shadow of nuclear weapons, but for generations yet unborn in every nation on Earth and, we believe, beyond Earth. They gave us, in brief, a glimpse of Mutually Assured Survival.

To deprive our more tendentious critics of a straw man to knock over, we emphasize once again, what Assured Survival does not and cannot mean. While it does, once implemented, assure the continued existence of all peoples, and increase the chance of that existence being a peaceful one, it does not—no strategy can—provide perfect assurance of the survival of everyone, or of any one person. Terrorists might one day detonate a nuclear weapon inside a city; it is also conceivable that a missile, or several missiles, might be fired through error or insanity on the part of some local commander; nuclear-tipped ballistic missiles might still be unleashed in general warfare—but with Assured Survival in place, most of these dreadful weapons, perhaps almost all, would be intercepted. The casualties of such a war would probably be unequalled in human history—but at *the very least, scores of millions of people would survive who, without a defensive umbrella, would have died.* What is the dollar value of fifty million lives?

It is absurd to demand that a system save 100% of the people in its care, to demand that no defensive umbrella be developed unless it be guaranteed to intercept *every* hostile weapon. No rational physician would claim 100% certainty that an operation would be successful for every patient; no rational designer of automobile restraint systems would claim that his system assures the survival of every user. The operation and the restraint system should, however, assure the survival of many, and better the chances of all.

Strategists ignore the defensive aspects of war at their peril. From Sun Tzu to Clausewitz, the best strategy analysts have always regarded the defense as "the stronger form of war." Hannibal was a master at combining defense with offense. The French won at the Marne through counter-offensive strategy.

Stalin regarded the counter-offensive as the most significant form of war, and to this day the Strategic Defense Forces are a separate branch of service in the Soviet Union, taking precedence over the Soviet Air Force and the Soviet Navy. The Defense Forces are a separate and unified combat organization, reporting directly to the Supreme Commander. They are always commanded by a Marshal of the Soviet Union. The Soviet Army (Land Forces) is five times the size of the Strategic Defense Force, but is headed only by a General of the Army.

It is high time that U.S. strategists, including academic theoreticians, rediscover strategic defense; to reject defensive systems on the grounds that they are imperfect is absurd. Assured Survival cannot assure the survival of any particular individual, but it can provide assurance that many more individuals, and society itself, will survive. To demand absolute perfection from fallible humanity is to demand the unattainable, and those who demand the unattainable are not to be taken seriously.

Once it was popular to characterize an impossible demand as "asking for the Moon." Now, Americans have landed on the Moon, and we stand ready to return. With clearer vision we could have gone from our lunar demonstrations to more practical developments. In later chapters, we will show how the Moon will be of great importance in ending the terrible threat of nuclear war.

CHAPTER TWO

Defense: High-Tech or Now-Tech?

Serious analysts of technology agree that there is not, and never will be, an ultimate weapon. A Soviet military affairs analyst, writing in *Communist of the Armed Forces* in September, 1974, said, ". . . there can be no limit to the application of [natural] laws in technological designs. From this point of view, any, the most terrible, weapon cannot be called absolute since in its stead can come a still more powerful one."

More recently and much more to the point, U.S. Defense strategist Ronald Lehman II was quoted in *Businessweek* as saying, "There's always a better system on the drawing board. But there comes a time when you have to decide, and we're approaching it now." Senator Malcom Wallop, in the same article, replied ". . . so let's get on with it." *(Businessweek,* 20 June 1983). The Senator and Lehman were referring specifically to the choice of systems for Global Ballistic Missile Defense (GBMD).

In 1957, the outstanding Soviet physicist Peter Kapitza declared that large-scale defenses against ballistic missiles were not only feasible, but inevitable; the Soviets long ago decided that they must "get on with it," proceeding to develop elements which may soon be melded into a GBMD system.

It is instructive, if frightening, to list a few Soviet advances with missile defense firmly in mind. They are deploying immense, hardened long-range radars deep inside the Soviet Union. As stated previously, while radars near the border are allowed by the ABM treaty, interior radars, which are obviously for ABM systems, are a flagrant violation. They have flight-tested a small lifting body which could be piloted for maneuvering both in space and within the atmosphere. Their directed-energy weapons research is in some respects advanced beyond ours and is clearly directed against both satellites and ballistic missiles. Perhaps most significant, Soviet cosmonauts have become almost a constant manned presence in space, amassing far more experience than we have. These developments are richly suggestive of a Soviet GBMD program aimed at permanent manned space stations, manned orbital interceptors with reentry capability, an integrated ground-based radar system to aid intercept of our missiles, and space-based beam weapons which could destroy anything that ventures beyond the atmosphere. For them, the missile defense systems we label as "high-tech" are much nearer to being "now-tech."

In March of 1983, President Reagan announced his Administration's decision to embark on a GBMD program (fortunately, the acronym DABM, i.e., Defense Against Ballistic Missiles has been abandoned. As one Air Force general put it, "I don't want to dab 'em, I want to ZAP 'em.") The Administration's next step was to form a blue-ribbon steering committee under the auspices of Defense Secretary Caspar Weinberger. Among the primary aims of this committee was to decide, with all deliberate speed, which hardware systems should be developed.

Our Councils's Systems Assessment Group report was only one set of recommendations to be considered.

Some analysts favor off-the-shelf systems in the interests of quick system deployment, while others favor more advanced systems which promise higher effectiveness, but with higher attendant costs in both time and money. Simply put, Weinberger's committee had to weigh (among many other things) "hightech" against "now-tech."

As a direct result of "economies" in military and other R&D in the 70's, we have very little "nowtech" hardware for Assured Survival. But at least we do have some systems that could be quickly adapted to provide the "top" layer of a multilayer GBMD.

Layered Defense

The layered approach has been thoroughly covered in Graham's *High Frontier* (Tor Books, 1983). The first layer would be composed of several hundred orbital "trucks," each of which would carry about forty small, self-propelled devices, each of which would intercept an ICBM—or for that matter, a shorter-range missile targeted against an ally—during that missile's booster phase.

While accelerating in boost phase, a rocket emits enough infrared (IR) radiation to permit current sensors to provide guidance to intercept. The ABM missile would explode and spread a cylinder of pellets, roughly akin to a shotgun blast, in the path of the ascending missile. This layer could account for many, though certainly not all, of an ICBM salvo by destroying them miles above the Earth—but relatively near their own launch sites; and they would quickly fall back to their country of origin. Aside from providing a pleasing esthetic symmetry for defense strategists, it would be a deterrent to any first strike planner.

The satellite truck with self-propelled devices was first proposed by Fred "Bud" Redding as an example of a defensive system that can be taken "off the shelf." It requires no advances in the state of the art of propulsion, tracking, or guidance. Deployment could begin soon after a "go" decision. Given determination and a Presidential priority, a partially effective—

far from leak proof—defensive system *could be in place within five years.*

The specific system originally proposed by Redding is probably not optimum, but it is feasible. The concept of anti-missile defense from satellites can be implemented in many different ways, with various kill mechanisms on different orbits, different guidance systems on different frequencies, and with smaller or larger numbers of satellite carriers. It matters far less *which* system is chosen than that *a* system *is* chosen, and *soon.*

The Soviet Union uses a technological strategy of deploying minimum systems, then upgrading and improving them steadily. The result begins with less than optimum equipment, but ends with solid results—and crews trained to use the new systems. Although we should never slavishly imitate the Soviets, we could do worse than adopt that element of their approach to our own strategic defense.

One advantage of an Earth-circling orbital system plus extended-range Sidewinder missiles is that they would defend not just us, but our allies. Both NATO and Japan would benefit. This effort could begin *immediately* as an alliance-wide enterprise. There is no reason why our allies should not bear part of the costs, since they would certainly benefit from the results. At present, the security of Europe rests in MAD. Surely a rational European would trade such a doubtful deterrent for a real defense.

Mid Range

A second layer of defensive satellites would be orbited later, pending further development of sensors. Our IR sensors cannot, at present, reliably track a nuclear warhead during the later, unpowered portion of its trajectory because its infrared emissions are very much lessened. We are, however, making steady progress toward this goal, and many key elements of the system can be deployed now. This second layer might employ directed energy weapons for their kill mechanism, since high-energy lasers are already in advanced development and should be deployable by the time our advanced sensors are ready. Many of the warheads that filtered past our first (kinetic energy kill) layer would be accounted for by the second layer.

Terminal Interception

A third layer, in terms of the sequence of intercepts, would be based not in space, but near hardened targets on our own soil. This third layer is termed "point defense", and would be designed to defeat incoming warheads (called "reentry vehicles", or RVs, since bombs are contained in special structures for reentry into the Earth's atmosphere) by intercepting them within a few miles of their targets. The point defended by this system would typically be a number of missile silos hardened to survive a nuclear explosion a thousand feet distant. Thus, even if the warheads are "salvage fused" to detonate if intercepted, very few will perform their intended missions. The awareness by a potential aggressor that very few warheads would succeed, and that therefore counterstrike would be certain and devastating, is a powerful deterrent to that aggressor.

Point Defense Systems

We could begin deployment of this point-defense system immediately. Since this ground-based layer defends specific points, we can employ a relatively simple and inexpensive radar, searching a small "threat cone" through which an RV with its nuclear warhead must pass. Our point defense weapons need only be able to saturate small threat cones at the proper moment.

In response to the threat posed by the Soviet Union's massive tank battalions, we already have at least one fully-developed weapon which could be quickly adapted from its original role, the General Electric GAU-8 gun, a minicannon of extremely high fire-rate— several *thousand* 30 mm. rounds per minute. The GAU-8 is the chief armament of our A-10 attack aircraft, and was developed for infantry support against tanks. The GAU-8's firepower is astonishing; assailed by many hundreds of these projectiles, each over an inch in diameter, a tank is simply obliterated. It occurred to personnel at Eglin AFB that saturating a small volume containing a tank was in many respects analogous to saturating a threat cone containing a nuclear warhead.

In terms of its proposed new mission, the GAU-8 is dirt cheap; its projectiles are non-nuclear; and any one of these projectiles would deliver enough kinetic energy to do the job. Deployed as a point defense, the gun would employ simple, expendable range-only radars and could be protected in a hardened installation. Assuming that the target was a Soviet RV carrying a 500 kt (half-megaton) warhead our missiles will survive an air burst roughly 1,000 from their silos. The GAU-8's range is at least 8,000 feet; provided with radar guidance, the gun would saturate the threat cone so thoroughly that the RV kill probability for a single gun is roughly 90%. The gun is so inexpensive that we could deploy more than one for each silo and command site. Two would have a kill rate of 99%. Three, 99.9 and so on. Unfortunately, the guns themselves are vulnerable to salvage-fused warheads, so their effectiveness could not be counted on for multiple waves of ICBMs—but they would ensure the survivability of our missiles long enough for a launch. And the Russians would know it.

A GAU-8 point defense system could operate automatically since it uses short-range non-nuclear projectiles, and could be in place very soon after the go-ahead decision. Because the existing ABM treaty defines an ABM system in terms of missiles and launchers, it can be convincingly argued that the ABM treaty does not prohibit this minicannon; in any event we are permitted one defensive system.

Though later versions of this system would doubtless yield even higher confidence of point defense, the GAU-8 is an excellent example of now-tech, ready for application to Assured Survival. A GAU-8 based point defense would be cheap and easy. Surely we can begin deployment *now*.

Beyond the GAU-8 other point defense systems are already under study. They typically would employ high-acceleration rockets directed by various radar emplacements. Rather than replacements, they can, at least initially, be thought of as extensions of the GAU-8's.

One system studied by Vought Corporation would use a derivative of the Lance missile carrying many small flechette warheads for a kinetic energy kill. The payload would be a half-ton, sufficient to saturate a threat cone with arrow-like projectiles. This system is envisioned for the defense of cities as well as missile silos.

Tracor MBA, in a study of silo point defense, proposes to saturate a threat cone with swarms of small, spin-stabilized rockets accelerating to mile-per-second velocity, the volleys repeated at roughly one-second intervals until perhaps 10,000 very small projectiles have been fired. The "Swarmjet" system would use hardened recoilless launchers with high confidence that a single stike by a projectile (perhaps two inches in diameter and a foot in length) would destroy a warhead a mile from the silo. Its proponents liken it to slamming a steel door in the face of an incoming missile.

The target tracking for the Swarmjet, and for some other point defense systems, would be by trilateration of rather simple, cheap range-only radars. A silo would be surrounded at a distance of a few miles by three arrays of four radars each. The wide dispersal of radar emplacements assures that one warhead could destroy only one emplacement, permitting the radar system to continue operation. Since these radars do not need to acquire a target beyond 40,000 foot altitude, they would be relatively unaffected by very-high-altitude re-entry effects. Also, with this radar dispersal scheme, radars can look around the detonation of a salvage-fuzed RV in order to track other RVs that may follow. Trilateration of low-cost, range-only radars would require an aggressor to expend several RVs for reasonable confidence of destroying a single target.

Sandia National Laboratory has studied a conceptually similar system that would defend silos using range-only radars in a trilateration scheme to aim unguided, non-nuclear rockets which would be detonated into a threat cone.

The Army's LoADS (for Low Altitude Defense System) has obtained enough funding for initial development of some hardware. Like the earlier Sprint ABM, LoADS can carry a nuclear warhead and would be capable of very high accelerations. A slender cone in shape, somewhat less than twenty feet long and roughly four feet in diameter at its base, a LoADS interceptor would be capable of abrupt maneuvers so that it could even intercept a maneuvering RV. The intercept would, as its name implies, be made at an altitude under 50,000 feet and while non-nuclear warheads have been designed, in its role as a silo defense weapon the LoADS interceptor would probably carry a nuclear warhead of low yield—a few tens of kilotons. This warhead, though its yield is low in terms of shock, would have a neutron fluence so high that if detonated anywhere near the incoming RV, it could saturate the fissionable material in the RV warhead, rendering it unable to detonate. The LoADS interceptor would not need to "hit a bullet with a bullet", it would be lethal to an RV if detonated within several hundred feet of its target. It would be more conceptually similar to hitting a fly with a fly swatter.

Intercepting a nuclear warhead some miles above the ground, LoADS would prevent a megaton-range explosion at or near ground level; it would exchange the enemy's planned very big, very "dirty" ground-level detonation for the interceptor's very small, very "clean" medium-altitude detonation. (As early as the 1960s from "Plowshare" studies of peaceful uses of nuclear detonations we knew that warheads could be designed with minimal residual radioactivity.)

Naturally, this exchange would defeat the enemy RV missions. Furthermore, the LoADS vehicle would make a successful intercept even if its accuracy was slightly impaired, indeed even if the enemy RV was maneuvering in some terminal guidance scheme. Finally, mathematical analysis reveals that even if LoADS proved to be relatively inefficient, failing intercept half the time, it would still extract such a high price in enemy RVs that the aggressor would probably find the targets not worth the cost. Since the targets would be our counter-strike force, this is not very different from saying that an aggressor would find a first strike not worth the cost.

But LoADS has disadvantages, too. It would be a complex, expensive system and could not soon be deployed despite the previous systems-development work by such companies as McDonnell-Douglas, Raytheon, and TRW. Also, because of its small nuclear warhead, it would probably be constrained by special high-level "release" signals which are not required for conventional defensive weapons.

LoADS has received a great deal of study and many more details of the factors involved in the assessment of LoADS, including deceptive basing of the interceptors, their site hardening, and so on are available. Further discussion on LoADS, various other point defense schemes, and missile basing in general can be found in the unclassified volume of the 1981 document, *MX Missile Basing*, which was prepared by the Office of Technology Assessment.

Beam Weapons

So far we have only talked about weapons based on traditional tried-and-true kill mechanisms. None of these systems is very efficient; whatever means we propose to use to drive a chunk of metal or a shower of neutrons into a target which is moving at hypersonic velocity, we will squander a great deal of energy to assure that we deliver a relatively small amount of energy against that target. We also take certain risks when we employ such weapons in the vicinity of our own assets; a shotgun blast isn't selective. Neither is a fireball.

A beam device, however, is the most exquisitely selective weapon since blackmail. A narrow beam of directed energy can travel at or near the speed of light—six orders of magnitude (one million times) faster than a bullet—so the fire control system does not need to "lead" the target or to unleash energy in a broad pattern in hopes that a small percentage of that energy will strike the target. A tightly focused laser, fired from a space-based GBMD system, can traverse over a thousand miles of space in less than a hundredth of a second to deliver a tremendous burst of energy against a small portion of a fast-moving target, and gut it.

The tremendous potential of directed energy weapons had gained them some strong adherents, but for years U.S. beam-weapon research proceeded without any coordinated effort to develop their anti-ICBM role. Then on the last day of October, 1977, Lockheed's Dr. Maxwell Hunter finished an unclassified paper he had prepared at home. Hunter had spent two years on the National Space Council during the Kennedy and Johnson administrations and knew where his now-famous "Halloween" paper might be well-received among defense planners. Hunter's paper is reprinted in this book (see Appendix) both for its clear exposition of the issue and for its historic value.

Wyoming's Senator Malcolm Wallop read Hunter's paper and recognized its impeccable reasoning, then urged Hunter to develop his thesis with several other proponents of beam weapons. Acting as private citizens, and without the official approval of their respective companies (Charles Stark Draper Laboratory, Lockheed, Perkin-Elmer, and TRW), these men briefed a dozen U.S. senators on the classified details of orbiting beam-weapon schemes. So far so good; but when they advocated their ideas to military officers already committed to less sophisticated BMD systems, the response was resentment bordering on rage. Catapult designers must have felt the same outrage when cannoneers first encroached on their turf.

The four civilians gained a certain notoriety and the wry designation, "Gang of Four"; but the gang quickly disbanded to avoid further repercussions against their companies (which, we hasten to emphasize, had not officially sponsored any of the briefings). Yet any relief felt by the resentful generals could not have lasted long. Several senators, now thoroughly aware of the possibilities of beam-weapon defenses, began to press for a strategic shift away from MAD. Some encouragement was also forthcoming from military weaponeers who, of course, had not *all* regarded beam weapon missile defenses with hostility. The research that gave Hunter and others their expertise had been largely funded with the cognizance of believers in the Pentagon. Exactly as envisioned by Hunter's Gang of Four, the strategic shift would involve serious analysis of beam weapons and expanded funding for these so-called "star wars" systems.

Proponents of beam weapons tend to wince when media attach the "star wars" label to their designs because critics invented and apply the term in an attempt to trivialize developments they regard as fanciful or flatly impossible. And some of those same critics deride high-tech developments as fanciful until the day after the new technology becomes commercially available. Wrist calculators, home computers with built-in telephone modems, and laser target designators for sporting rifles were dismissed as fanciful "star-wars" schemes as recently as the last few years by technologically conservative critics. All are readily available today. Some GBMD proponents embrace the star wars label rather like the American colonists embraced "Yankee Doodle." They say that star wars is a term implying advanced technology and near-future availability.

Because laser rangefinders and target designators are now installed on U.S. tanks, the most ardent critic must accept them as operational hardware. It is still possible to disdain the effectiveness of high energy lasers (HELs), however, because these systems are still in the research and development arena. Most of the details of the new HEL systems are classified, but chemically powered HEL weapons have been installed in a military version of the Boeing 707. Small rocket-powered missiles have been destroyed in flight by HEL. And in Nevada, underground tests proved that the tremendous fluence of x-rays emitted from a small nuclear device can be focused into an array of x-ray lasers capable of destroying numerous targets simultaneously and from a great distance.

The experiments listed above are only a few examples of current U.S. beam-weapon technology. A complete list would describe other methods, in addition to chemical and nuclear, for pumping a laser; and other types of beams including microwaves and particle beams, which employ "kill mechanisms" somewhat different from most lasers. We will discuss the most promising of these systems, as they relate to ballistic missile defense, in the following pages.

Beam Weapon Systems

In the U.S., laser weapons have received more funding than other types of directed energy weapons such as particle beams, so they are likely to be the first high-energy beam weapons to become operational in this country. We may not be the first country to develop HELs, however. A prominent U.S. laser expert warns that Soviet military laser programs are funded several times better than ours; that those programs have been underway for a long time; and that they are directed by Nobel laureates.

The ideal environment for a laser weapon is space. So much energy flows along a HEL beam that dust notes and air molecules within the beam's path will literally explode. This property of HELs has prompted studies of laser *propulsion* systems by a few noted investigators, e.g., Forward, Kantrowitz, and Myrabo. We can draw comfort from this potentially peaceful use of HELs, but detonation of particles in the path of a laser beam can seriously impede its progress.

At lower energy densities, a HEL can still provoke combustion or significant heating of particles in its path. This yields a "thermal bloom" phenomenon (among others) which can defocus the narrow beam unless the system employs adaptive optics to account for such effects. Adaptive optics are under development but, they add to the system's cost and complexity. No wonder, then, that some designers argue for space-based HEL systems, where there are no atmospheric effects to fight.

Space-based Chemical Lasers

A typical space-based HEL system would employ large lasers on orbiting satellites, obtaining power from reactions of chemicals carried onboard and directing the beam with a primary mirror. Physically, the largest part of the system would be the laser cavity and the tanks containing the chemical fuel reactants. The mirror would be somewhat smaller, perhaps four meters in diameter; and smaller still would be the target tracking/pointing system which aims the mirror. Each of these would require lifting some twenty tons of mass into orbit— not cheap, but easily within our present capability.

This HEL battle station would be highly vulnerable to enemy action unless it were armored. The armor might comprise layers of material to resist damage from metal fragments or from HEL impingement. The development of such armor will probably parallel the history of armored tanks, with countermeasures and counter-countermeasures that do not, however, cancel the value of the armored vehicle. Indeed, within a few years, HEL battle stations could be encased in virtually impregnable armor made from lunar regolith, or asteroidal materials, which, curiously, can be brought into position more cheaply than equivalent amounts could be lifted from Earth.

The power of this HEL, based on designs proposed

by Lockheed and TRW for demonstration within the next few years, would be about five megawatts. It could focus on an ICBM in boost phase 1,000 miles distant and deliver 300 watts per square centimeter against the missile's thin hide as the ICBM climbed out of the atmosphere. Two seconds or less of this kind of attention would cause catastrophic failure of a liquid-propellant missile, unless the missile were armored (which would make it too heavy for long-range trajectory). Feasibility demonstration of the Lockheed-TRW system would cost $3.5 or $4 billion.

Several other ideas have been suggested to reduce the vulnerability of thin-skinned ICBMs to far-distant lasers. The huge missile could be made to spin during its boost phase, which would spread the laser heat over a wider area, reducing the energy density impinging against a given spot on the missile. Yet this would, at best, yield a three-or four-fold reduction in delivered energy density; not a sure "fix" and, in any case, imparting a spin to these missiles would create *serious* problems in aerodynamics and guidance. Designers, scrambling for some logical counter against beam weapons, have also suggested entirely new ICBM designs of high acceleration, which achieve boost-phase burnout while still at low altitude. Thus the missile's identifying "signature" would cease while still in the atmosphere.

Such high acceleration systems are not invulnerable to the next generation of flourine/deuterium lasers, which can reach through many miles of atmosphere. In addition, a missile achieving burnout within the atmosphere will be so heated by atmospheric friction that it will almost undoubtedly be detectable by distant IR sensors once it reaches space.

All of these ideas for reducing missile vulnerabilities miss the point in any event. If the Soviets are forced to scrap their present fleet of ICBMs and deploy brand new ones that spin, or have super acceleration, the U.S. will already have achieved a significant strategic goal. Any reduction in the numbers of systems threatening us is desirable; to force the Soviets to scrap their highly expensive ICBM fleet and deploy another would be worth a very high price indeed.

In fact, it is unlikely that the Soviets have the economic resources to deploy a new ICBM fleet. At present they have four ICBM production lines working three shifts daily. Construction of these missiles and their production facilities has nearly bankrupted the Soviet economy; a requirement to start over would very likely produce economic collapse. Certainly it would be many years before the Soviets could regain the significant strategic superiority they now enjoy.

The Soviet Union is not a wealthy nation. They have hardly a hundred miles of paved roads between their major cities. Their economy is stalemated, saddled with a system whose inefficiency would be incredible if it were not well known. Their only claim to the status of "super power" is their weapons, and they have devoted a large part of their GNP to producing them. This is not a feat they are likely to be able to repeat.

Even if the Soviets were to design and deploy a new ICBM fleet using less vulnerable rockets, more megawatts, or a larger mirror, provide a more potent HEL. The larger the mirror, the more tightly a beam can be focused farther from the mirror. A few critics, more prominent than knowledgeable, have objected that mirrors of this size are beyond our current technology, perhaps forgetting that a sixteen-foot mirror has been in place at Mt. Palomar for fifty years. A more credible criticism might be that, beyond a certain size, traditional mirrors would be difficult to lift into orbit. Answers to this include segmenting the mirror, and making it of material less unwieldy than glass. The mirror is not intended for such elegant purposes as studying distant galaxies; its reflectivity must be high but its resolution need not match that of the world's finest telescopes.

A chemical laser gets its power from chemical reactions. One design burns methane and nitrogen trifluoride. Atomic fluorine is thereby released, flow-ing through nozzles into a chamber where hydrogen is injected to react with the fluorine. The resulting hydrogen fluoride molecules, highly excited, emit infrared radiation—similar to the heat waves of a 'heat lamp,' though enormously more intense—at a wavelength of 2.7 micrometers. Internal mirrors within the laser cavity direct this energy to the large primary aiming mirror, which focuses the beam on a distant target. This wavelength, incidentally, is strongly absorbed by Earth's atmosphere so that aircraft in flight would probably be safe from this particular beam.

By substituting deuterium for ordinary hydrogen, however, we obtain an IR wavelength of 3.8 micrometers which is not so quickly absorbed by the atmosphere. Such a device could be effective against aircraft—perhaps even against ground targets.

We might obtain complete GBMD coverage with fifty of these orbiting battle stations. Or we might increase the mirror size and power output so that fewer stations are required, though each would be more expensive. In one clever adaptation, designers propose relay mirrors in orbit which would gather and refocus beams from distant orbiting HEL battle stations, thus reducing the number and cost of orbiting stations, as well as allowing the battle stations to be positioned in higher less vulnerable orbits.

Such a system would be expensive, and until protected by massive armor the stations would be attractive targets, just as an aircraft carrier is an attractive target. But also like the vulnerable carrier, the HEL battle station could defend itself in a formidable manner, sharing mutual support with others of its kind. Furthermore the Soviets would have the same disincentives regarding attacking an American battle station as hold for our naval vessels.

Ground Based Lasers and Space Relay Mirrors

If we could save money by orbiting inexpensive relay mirrors to improve our coverage, why not leave *all* the laser hardware, including the fuels and pri-

mary mirrors, on the ground while orbiting only the
relay mirrors? Critics immediately point to atmospheric effects, but the GBL (Ground-Based Laser)
has advantages that may overcome atmospheric
impedance.

To begin with, the GBL is easily and cheaply acces-
sible for maintenance, modification, and refueling.
We need not expend huge sums toward a slight upgrading of system reliability because, when something goes wrong with the laser, we can rush to fix it
in a pickup truck—not a space shuttle. We can also
install much more powerful lasers on the ground
than in space. Weight is not a critical problem; and
of course the laser installation can be deep inside a
mountain for maximum site hardening. Also, a
ground-based system can employ available electrical
power instead of stored chemical fuels.

As for atmospheric phenomena: we could generate
a beam so powerful that it simply forces its way
through dust and water vapor, or we could produce
laser beams in visible or ultraviolet wavelengths. We
would also choose emplacement sites where clear
weather was the rule, following the logic and tactics
of astronomers with their observatories.

The unaided ground-based laser is, however, quite
limited. Even on a mountaintop, such a laser could
not reach out several thousand miles to interdict a
rising missile because the Earth is simply in the
way. We need platforms that are hundreds of miles
high—perhaps a few that are many thousands of
miles high—to provide line-of-sight coverage of all
possible targets. Physicist George Keyworth, pivotal
Science Advisor to President Reagan, has noted with
optimism that mirrors at various orbital heights can
provide a layered GBMD. This is where orbiting relay mirrors can play an important role.

The relay mirrors receive the laser beam, and can
actually correct distortions created in the beam while
it was passing through the atmosphere. These are
the adaptive optics, which (very clearly unlike a rigid
astronomical lens) can change their shape to pre-

cisely cancel distortions in the initial beam. One similar scheme, incidentally, is to maintain a continuous low-power beam from the orbiting relay mirror to the ground-based laser—a particularly straightforward task if the relay mirror is in equatorial geosynchronous orbit, always above the laser. The distortion of the continuous beam is measured on the ground, which permits constant monitoring of atmospheric distortion. The adaptive optics can then be on the ground as well, preshaping the high-power beam so that, when the HEL fires, the orbiting relay mirror receives a corrected, undistorted beam. The relay mirror, from its lofty position, can reach out thousands of miles with the focused beam.

Relay mirrors, lifted into known orbits, would be known targets for hostile action. (They would also, of course, be relatively inexpensive and indisputable tripwires. If several of our relay mirrors indicated failure within a few minutes, we would ascribe it to probable hostile action.) That's why some designers prefer "pop-up" relay mirrors. The term "pop-up" does not refer to underground hardware which pops to the surface, but rather to hardware which can be quickly lifted from the Earth's surface to orbital heights. For example, a relay mirror could be the payload of an old Polaris missile, carried in a small submarine and then "popped up" from underwater to its fighting height above the atmosphere.

These pop-up mirrors need not be in true orbits to perform a missile defense function. Because the pop-up mirror's booster would not provide enough velocity for orbit, the mirror would follow a ballistic trajectory of its own, keeping its orientation vis-a-vis parent GBLs and, necessarily, any targets that came into view. While each pop-up mirror would be useful for no longer than several minutes, we could launch additional mirrors for a sustained GBMD operation, using otherwise obsolete boosters for the job.

Two types of laser show the greatest promise for GBL systems, the excimer and the free-electron laser.

Both types would emit beams in visible or ultraviolet wavelengths, minimizing atmospheric effects.

The excimer, or rare gas/halide laser, is pumped by an electron beam and thus uses electrical power rather than chemicals for its energy source. The electron beam is injected into a laser cavity containing a rare gas, such as krypton, and a halogen gas, such as fluorine. The energy of the electron beam ionizes the fluorine, causing it to react with the krypton to form an unstable compound: krypton fluoride. This kind of unstable compound is called an excited dimer, or excimer. The excimer molecules then emit laser energy; in the case of krypton fluoride, at an ultraviolet wavelength of 0.248 micrometers. Western Research has designed a xenon chloride laser, for increased duration of HEL pulses. It should be fairly simple to generate extremely high-power beams by combining the outputs of numerous, relatively small excimer lasers.

A free-electron laser (FEL) also uses an electron beam instead of chemicals. The beam passes through a set of "wiggler" magnets which literally shake the electrons up and down in their passage, generating the laser beam. The energy of the electrons, and the spacing of the magnets, determine the wavelength of the laser. One potential advantage of the FEL, whether employed as a weapon or for other purposes, is that the system is tunable, and thus capable of emitting beams at different frequencies. It can also be aimed without mirrors.

Ground-based lasers would probably not emit continous beams, but would propagate a series of very short-duration pulses. A pulsed HEL, instead of simply heating part of the surface of a target ICBM with a continuous beam, would hammer that surface with repeated thermal shock. This extremely rapid heating via high-energy pulses tends to vaporize the surface of the target material, blowing it away as if a small explosive charge had been detonated at that point. The shock wave in the material penetrates into the material and destroys it.

Nuclear Explosive-Driven Beam Technologies

In testimony before congressional groups, experts generally agree that short-wavelength lasers (radiating at wavelengths below one micron), such as those in the extreme UV (ultraviolet) and X-ray range, have intrinsic military advantages over lasers of longer wavelength. However, most known chemical lasers radiate in the three-to-ten micron range, though some FELs and excimers boast short wavelengths. The controversy arises in choosing now-tech or high-tech, because chemical lasers are more highly developed while other laser pumping methods have more eventual promise. The most energetic laser of all would be one which focused some useful fraction of a nuclear bomb's short-radiation energy.

Beam weapons energized by nuclear explosions, collectively called "third generation systems," are under development at Lawrence Livermore and Los Alamos National Laboratories. Normally, a nuclear bomb generates an appalling amount of energy, but that energy is not focused; it radiates more or less spherically from the explosion. Much of this energy is released in the form of X-rays which, in the atmosphere, are absorbed by air molecules. These heated molecules in turn emit IR wavelengths as well as visible light, and generate a vast shock wave. So much X-ray energy is released that if even a small part of it can be focused the intensity of the resulting X-ray laser beam would beggar comparison with current lasers.

Proof of this principle has already been demonstrated in underground Nevada tests. Nobel laureate Hans Bethe is rather pessimistic about most GBMD schemes; according to him, a nuclear-driven laser GBMD system is the only one that makes scientific sense. Visiting Edward Teller in 1983 at Lawrence Livermore, Bethe found the studies and designs commendable. He noted, at the same time, that the present state of this concept is a long way from an operational weapon.

In another scheme, a nuclear-driven excimer could consist of an optical cavity between a pair of mirrors of perhaps two-meter apertures. X-rays produced by the explosion would pump excimer gases through the side of the optical cavity. Lasers would be arranged around the periphery of the bomb. The X-ray energy, colliding with the excimer gases, would generate high-energy electrons, providing pumping energy for the laser.

Still another design features metal plasma lasers formed from thin metal rods which are electrically vaporized just prior to the nuclear detonation, or may be vaporized by X-rays from the explosion itself. The X-rays excite the metal vapor, producing a "traveling wave" of ionized metal gas which emit coherent X-rays along the axis of the rod. This single-pass laser emission process, which can be produced only when the laser medium has a very high gain, is called a super-radiant laser. The energy of this X-ray pulse lasts only nanoseconds—billionths of a second—but during that time it can deliver a thousand kilocalories per square centimeter against a target.

The penetration of materials by X-rays creates a special problem for mirrors designed to reflect X-ray energy. Most of the "hardest," shortest waves would not be reflected by known materials but "soft" X-rays can be efficiently reflected. In one technique the rays are reflected at very shallow angles, termed a grazing incidence. Another mirror scheme uses alternate layers of materials of very different dielectric properties; this "cake" can reflect roughly half of the soft X-ray energy impinging on it. Thus, while much of the X-ray energy of a nuclear explosion would be unusable, the fraction which *can* be harnassed is still staggering.

Any laser pumped by nuclear explosion is not going to laze very long. In the sequence of operation the small nuclear device would detonate, energizing the laser for a brief but prodigiously powerful X-ray pulse; and instantly afterward, superheated gas from the bomb would convert the laser to superheated gas as well. Obviously this device can be used only once; yet *it can generate many simultaneous beams.*

In order to engage many simultaneous targets, multiple lasers would be positioned around the nuclear bomb. Each laser unit would track its own target missile or, if the device has more lasers than targets, lasers could be doubled up on a given target. ('Overkill' takes on a new and wonderful meaning here.) When the bomb is triggered, each laser fires one lethally powerful pulse. Thus a single small nuclear bomb could pump enough lasers to yield the simultaneous kill of perhaps fifty ICBMs. The cost of such a device would involve lasers, target tracking, and coordination in addition to the bomb, but the price of the single bomb is reputedly around $1 million. All aside from the salvation of people targeted by ICBMs, such a trade of assets is overwhelmingly in favor of the defense.

A nuclear-driven laser pulse can be in visible and ultraviolet wavelengths as well. Its kill mechanism is similar to that of the pulsed excimer and FEL, disrupting a target by the exceedingly fast rise-time of thermal shock against it. However, nuclear-driven HELs would operate in space, and could do so as pop-up systems lifted above the atmosphere on boosters, after warning that they would have targets within minutes.

Pop-up systems are effective against Sea Launched Ballistic Missiles (SLBMs). Since the warning time from launch of an SLBM until detonation over Washington is only twelve minutes, we have considerable incentive to deploy some means of increasing the warning time, and survivability of the President and other decision-makers.

Pop-up systems are less useful against ICBMs for the obvious reason that they cannot be employed against the missile in its boost phase, when it is easily detected, since the pop-up system is located far from the launch site. Given better IR sensors, pop-up nuclear pumped laser systems could be deployed in Canada and Alaska for mid-range intercept of cross polar ICBMs.

Nuclear pumped lasers are usually proposed for deployment as pop-up systems for several reasons. First, they are large and complex systems; permanent deployment in space would require periodic inspection and maintenance visits. There is also understandable reluctance to put nuclear materials in an unmanned and unguarded installation, even in space.

A second, often given, reason is that deployment of nuclear devices in space would abrogate treaties. This argument is spurious.

Certainly putting these devices in permanent orbit would require *renegotiation* of treaties. However, this will be required in any case.

Treaties are either concluded for a period (or a term), or they have cancellation clauses which provide that the signatories must give notice if they want to abrogate the agreed stipulations. For example, the ABM treaty may be cancelled by either side upon six months notice.

This point is important, since many critics of Assured Survival assert that we would have to break treaties if we were to go ahead with antiballistic defense; but it is not so. Termination of a treaty through the means specified within the treaty itself is no violation of international law or custom.

Treaties which deal with technology must be periodically updated in any case, or else they become either useless or dangerous for both sides. The Soviets will also want changes in the various treaties governing military uses of outer space. Notice can be given of intention either to terminate the treaty, or continue it only if amended.

Particle Beam Weapons

A particle beam (PB) comprises particles such as electrons, protons, or ions instead of the laser's radiant-energy photons. Some idea of the PB's effect is gained through the jargon of the trade; a particle beam is called a "bolt," as in "lightning bolt." It can fracture a target and burn a hole through it, causing secondary radiation in the target material which can disable any electronics in the target. Beams of neutral particles are dissipated by air, relegating their use mainly to space. Protons, embedded in an accelerated electron stream, have been fired as a proton beam and proton PBs of very much greater power seem practicable against targets within the atmosphere. It seems likely that a target struck by a PB within the atmosphere, whether it was struck while lumbering across a battlefield or while arrowing down from above, would be penetrated, disrupted inside, and shaken into uselessness by the physical impact of massive particles moving at velocities close to the speed of light.

Beams of neutral and charged particles show very great promise against targets that are too well-armored for attack by most lasers. For example, a hardened ground installation or a space-based asset protected by lunar slag armor might well survive repeated HEL strikes. Combinations of beams may also be employed for maximum effectiveness.

For over a decade, hundred-billion electron volt proton beams have been routinely generated both in the Soviet Union and in physics study centers in the West. FermiLab can generate proton beams of a *trillion* electron volts. There is no question that such a beam of atomic particles can be trained on a target; the challenge is in reducing the beam-generating facility to a compact package. A chilling aside: at present, much of our PB weapon research has been developed from work previously published by Soviet researchers.

At Los Alamos and Lawrence Livermore, the U.S. is researching PB technologies for both space and ground-based defensive systems. The White Horse neutral beam program at Los Alamos is studying a hydrogen ion source using a radio-frequency quadropole accelerator which, ironically, was first described in open scientific literature from previous Soviet research. There is considerable information in open literature regarding PBs as they relate to experiments in particle physics and fusion power research. The brief discussion here is one measure of the paucity of PB weapon developments in this country to date. At present, we must consider American PB weapons as residing in the most rarefied regions of the high-tech category, though our PB research is now receiving better funding in light of the more advanced Soviet work.

Information Technology

A thorough discussion of current and projected techniques for aiming weapons would require another book. Nevertheless, we must at least touch on them; they are crucial elements in the choices of defensive systems. The full panoply of information functions is implied by the term 'Command, Control, Communications and Intelligence' (C^3I), much of which relies on advances in electronics development. A fast-moving target must be detected and if possible identified; its probable path predicted; its implications fitted to other information available; and its countermeasures chosen—all this in the briefest possible time and with the maximum possible accuracy.

Radar technology is sufficiently advanced that, with canny placement and data linkage, various now-tech radars could serve some defensive systems as previously described. On the other hand, ground clutter and other interference seriously degrade the performance of radar which must look down from orbit to identify small moving targets. Ground-and aircraft-based radar, capable of seeing over obstacles and even over the horizon, are recent improvements which are still in advanced development.

Radar and other sensor techniques can be countered by such counter-countermeasures as nuclear bursts set off for the express purpose of blinding our sensors, and more work must be done to overcome these failure modes. A nuclear EMP also requires special hardening of vital communication electronics, and suggests that the opposite ends of the electromagnetic spectrum will both see greatly expanded development for C^3I. Extremely Low Frequency (ELF) and Very Low Frequency (VLF) wavelength transmissions are highly reliable even with nuclear detonations within the atmosphere. Their antennas must be very large, however, and those low frequencies mean very slow rates of transmitting messages. Extremely High Frequency (EHF) transmissions have different problems and different advantages. An EHF transmission, at 100 GigaHertz, can transmit messages at an extremely high rate. EHF antennas can be quite small, too, and the beam so highly directional that it is virtually undetectable by enemies. High-altitude nuclear bursts could cause 'scintillation', or ionosphere density fluctuations, that could bend the EHF beam for a few moments. In the C^3I arena as in other defensive technologies, the most likely route to success appears to be parallel developments; paving the high road and the low road simultaneously, as it were.

As we said earlier, the current state of the art in IR sensors permits us to track a hot object (such as a rising missile during its boost phase) with great precision. We can track it even from orbit with IR sensors. Background clutter is not a serious problem in this case because the target shines very brightly, compared to background IR. IR sensors require further development, however, before we can reliably track a rapidly cooling missile that is no longer trailing an infrared plume of rocket exhaust. We are now studying these advanced IR sensor techniques as well as UV sensor systems. But sensors only tell us what to expect; they are not, in themselves, countermeasures.

The countermeasure might be a radio frequency (RF) jamming technique, or a massive electromagnetic pulse (EMP). It might, on the other hand, be a searing laser pulse or repeated volleys of small metal projectiles. Some C^3I equipment is now capable of some of the support tasks for a GBMD system, while some other tasks cannot be adequately performed until we greatly improve the rates at which data can be transmitted with very high reliability.

Defense And Synergism

It seems clear to us that no single defensive system—not even one on the technical horizon—offers the same degree of assured survival that is offered by multiple-system concepts. Layered GBMD; active and passive (hardened) defenses; development of ELF and EHF communication systems; beam weapons with several basing schemes, with final aiming from various orbital distances: all are examples of synergism, systems that work together like bones and muscles to provide capabilities that no one system could match.

We find synergism, too, in the time dimension. We need assured survival always, but we cannot have advanced, operational defensive beam weapons for a decade to come. Point defense and orbital layers with kinetic energy weapons can, however, bridge the chronological gap for us. They will probably do so for the Soviets as well.

As long as we have one, it is not a bad thing that the Soviets also have a GBMD. Defensive shields possessed by both the Soviets and the West will probably yield a more stable peace than would a shield erected by only one side, since it would allay Soviet paranoia. We repeat that the Soviets, whatever their complaints against our GBMD, appear to be erecting one of their own without admitting it; in any event, for neither side to have a GBMD is not an option; *they* will have one. The question is, will we?

Expensive as it may be, a missile defense system will be far less expensive than the dollar value of New York, or Los Angeles, or Kansas City. Indeed, the entire cost of a GBMD system would not nearly match the funds we have spent in development of our offensive triad of bombers, ICBMs, and submarine-launched missiles.

Another benefit of defending ourselves can be inferred from the record of peaceful advances which would almost certainly have lagged, or proven impracticable, without spurring by military spending. The most obvious example of this is the global network of commercial air transport, which grew from American military air transport services during World War II. All over the globe, air traffic controllers and airline pilots speak English because the tremendous volume of peaceful air traffic, essential to conduct the world's business, largely remains the province of English-speaking people. What an economic tragedy for our nation if, a generation hence, space traffic controllers all speak Russian.

CHAPTER THREE

Warbirds

"If we can make these terrible weapons obsolete and irrelevant, then no price is too high."—**Congressman George Brown (D. Calif.) at the third annual L-5 Society Space Development Conference.**

The frequent objection to military defenses in space is that, on moral or tactical grounds, we should not "weaponize" space. Yet, as physicist John D.G. Rather, among others, points out, space has already been weaponized for over twenty-five years. Space is the medium for delivery of nuclear weapons.

To give an idea of just how weaponized space would be in the event of an all-out nuclear war, Dr. Rather posited a Soviet attack comprising 1,000 ICBMs, 800 SLBMs (Sea-Launched Ballistic Missiles), 700 IRBMs (Intermediate Range Ballistic Missiles), and 1,500 bombers carrying cruise missiles. The ballistic missiles alone total 2,500 and since many would carry several RVs apiece, their total nuclear RV count would be on the order of 10,000. This does not include cruise missiles, which fly near the ground and do not need to reenter the atmosphere. Other scenarios list various mixes of Soviet offensive missiles which, like our own, vary widely in range and throw weight. A missile which can carry multiple independently-targetable reentry vehicles (MIRVs) is said to have a high throw weight. Its primary advantage is that MIRVs can be released against several widely-separated targets, so that one ICBM of high throw weight could destroy enemy cities and silos hundreds of miles apart. An RV targeted against a hardened silo can penetrate reinforced concrete to destroy a target a hundred feet or more below the surface.

Ballistic Missile Flight Phases

The timing and sequence of events during the flight of a ballistic missile are crucial to the understanding of defensive systems. A ballistic missile's flight can most conveniently be separated into three phases: boost phase, while the rocket is actually firing, boosting its payload into trajectory; midcourse or coast phase, from the end of boost to reentry; and terminal phase, from the beginning of reentry into atmosphere until detonation of the warhead. Boost and terminal phases last some two to five minutes apiece; the midcourse phase lasts ten to twenty minutes.

Boost phase is a critical time for a ballistic missile. The missile is still at an altitude low enough to involve high aerodynamic loads from air resistance. If the skin or structure are weakened in any place for any reason, aerodynamic forces will tear the bird apart. Solid-fuel missiles are typically somewhat sturdier than liquid-fuel missiles, but the entire motor case of an operating solid-fuel rocket is highly pressurized. It can burst if damaged in any way.

If the rocket propulsion stops prematurely, a ballistic missile warhead simply will not have enough velocity to coast to its target. If the propulsion system is defeated early enough, the missile may fall on the territory of the country that launched it. Since such an early failure could drop several nuclear warheads onto the countryside of the launching nation, nuclear warheads are uniformly *not* armed, therefore cannot detonate, until the end of boost phase. Thus, a ballistic missile which is hit during boost phase will *not* cause a nuclear explosion. Nor would we want it to, even if it does land on enemy ground. It is the essential beauty of Mutual Assured Survival that once it is in place, killing the enemy's women and children is no longer necessary as a response—and thus becomes morally insupportable. "Kill Russian missiles, not Russian schoolgirls" would be an appropriate and inspiring slogan for the Age of Mutual Assured Survival.

Boost phase is the best time to detect, track, and attack a ballistic missile. The plume of fiery exhaust from a rocket nozzle during boost phase creates a tremendous IR signature, day or night. At night, the visible light of a large rocket plume is visible from many miles on the ground, and from thousands of miles in space. It is possible, however, for clouds or dust to block much of this IR signature during the early part of boost phase. Therefore our sensors might, in the worst case, not detect a missile until perhaps fifty seconds after launch. If destroyed during boost phase, the missile gives spectacular evidence; the defender need not wonder whether he has achieved a kill and can turn his attention to other warbirds. Though tracking is somewhat more difficult than detection, the problem is simplified in that the missile must follow a general trajectory for its warheads to hit a given area of the Earth. Every additional moment of tracking yields more specific information to identify the missile's intended target. The required trajectory from launch silo to target(s) is referred to as a "threat tube". Almost to the instant of detonation, if a defender can interdict a threat tube with sufficient energy at the right moment, that particular threat is ended.

It is theoretically possible to build a ballistic missile which has an extremely high acceleration, and which could reach its final burnout velocity after only twenty to fifty seconds. Such a missile would

still be within the atmosphere at burnout; the term
for this is "endoatmospheric burnout." If and when
such advanced missiles are developed, they would be
more difficult to track, though aerodynamic heating
of these missiles might provide an IR signature unless they discarded heat shields early in their trajectories.

At the end of the boost phase, the missile discards
the protective aerodynamic deployment shell from
its payload, and then performs final trim maneuvers
with star sightings (celestial navigation), or inertial
navigation systems. At this point, the warheads are
armed; we don't know if the Soviets use salvage
fuses, so named because they cause a warhead to
detonate if intercepted or disturbed in flight and so
"salvage" some of its usefulness. Certainly by the
time our country has significant ABM capability we
must assume the Soviets will be salvage-fusing their
warheads. And so what? Better a detonation in space
than the obliteration of a city.

During coast phase, the payload separates from
the empty booster. Though midcourse maneuvers will
cause portions of the missile payload to move away,
in general the entire system is coasting through its
trajectory at several miles per second. The discarded shroud, pieces of chaff, and perhaps lightweight inflatable decoys may interfere with defensive
radars seeking to track RVs. During this phase, current defensive systems are at maximum disadvan-
tage in identifying and tracking the RVs and their
warheads.

Terminal phase begins relatively near the target,
in the fringes of the upper atmosphere. Here, components not designed to penetrate the atmosphere, such
as boosters and lightweight decoys, are left behind to
be incinerated by atmospheric friction as the RVs,
aided by gravity and possibly by a terminal maneuvering system (a maneuverable reentry vehicle is
called a MaRV), streak toward their targets relatively unimpeded by the atmosphere.

*   *   *

Ballistic Missile Payloads

Without shielding in a very special container, a warhead hurled into ballistic trajectory would be incinerated by air friction as it reentered the atmosphere at 10,000 miles an hour. This container is the real reentry vehicle, but it is common practice to refer to the container and its warhead as a reentry vehicle, or RV.

The laws of aerodynamics force certain decisions on designers. Given roughly the same level of technology, Americans and Soviets alike will arrive at similar optimum penetration shapes for RVs. This can also be seen in the shape of the small Soviet aerobody, whose appearance can only be described as a vest-pocket Shuttle. (The same tacit unanimity on optimum shape can be seen in auto races like Le Mans, where some cars reach velocities of 100 meters per second. Many different prototype designs compete, and while aerodynamic advances distinguish a few of these machines, the most successful innovations are soon adopted by all the others. A high-tech Le Mans prototype can be identified virtually on sight, regardless of its country of origin.)

A late-model Soviet RV probably looks very much like our own, though sizes differ. The conical skin is thick and highly polished, like the graphite tip of some enormous pencil. The forward end of the cone is rounded rather than needle-sharp, because a sharp tip would be worn away during reentry anyhow, possibly in such a way as to deflect the RV from its deadly course. The RV skin ablates, or wears away, during reentry; thus much of the heat generated by reentry is not absorbed, but discarded with the fiery ablated particles. Observers describe RVs after hypersonic testing, at Arnold Engineering Development Center in Tennessee, as looking as though they had been roughly sandpapered by millions of particles of grit. The rounded RVs reveal the tremendous heat of the tests by varicolored oxide films which remain bonded to the noses, reminiscent of the rainbow hues of a knife blade tempered by a blacksmith. Of course an RV would be glowing during its last hypersonic moments before its nuclear payload detonated.

During the launch of a ballistic missile, its RVs are covered by an aerodynamic shell. The shell need not withstand ferocious ablation because the missile is slowly accelerating and does not reach miles-per-second velocity until it is in the tenuous outer edges of the atmosphere. Once into coast phase, as we said above, the missile sheds the shell surrounding its MIRVs.

A MIRV payload consists of several warhead/reentry vehicles attached to a "bus", which has its own small steering propulsion capability. After the missile's main propulsion system terminates, the bus fires its steering jets and then releases an RV at the proper moment for a given target. The bus then maneuvers again to aim another RV, releases that RV, and so on. Each conical RV may be up to four or five feet long and two or three feet in diameter.

The bus, however, initially carries all the RVs and while not very massive, it is fairly large—five to ten feet long by a six to ten foot diameter. In addition to its RVs, the bus may—and when U.S. ABM systems are in place must be expected to—carry radar-foiling chaff and decoys, "penetration aids" as they are called. Penetration aids will not fool point defenses because the heavy RVs "shed" the lightweight decoys at very high altitude because the decoys are much slowed by air friction. *Heavy* decoys seem unlikely—if you can afford the weight of a heavy decoy you can afford to add another RV! An RV, to damage a hardened target, must travel through a narrow threat cone which can be rapidly identified by defensive radars. It is impossible to overstate the importance of point defense—and the fact that we have *right now* weaponry that can be adapted to that end. Even the most ideologically blinkered proponent of *MAD*ness must admit the stabilizing effect of reducing our strategic forces' vulnerability.

We have some data on the explosive power or "yield" of various warheads carried by Soviet missiles:

SS-11 one 1.5 megaton
SS-13 one 1.0 megaton
SS-17 four 5.0 megaton
SS-18 eight(?) 2.0 megaton
SS-19 six 0.5 megaton
SS-20 three 0.15 megaton

As the guidance of RVs improves, MIRVs become still more attractive to offensive planners because several small accurate warheads can destroy more "assets" than one large warhead can. Because the blast and firestorm effects of a nuclear explosion diminish as a cube-root function, several widely spaced "small" explosions over a city could do more damage with less total energy yield than could a single explosion of very high yield. More to the point, as accuracy improves, smaller and so lighter warheads can take out the same hardened target.

While defensive weapons may be seen as deterrents, weapons of peace, ICBMs are undeniably weapons of war. If we are to deploy defensive systems, we should have a clear idea of the Soviet warbirds we must defend against, and to that end brief descriptions of those missiles follow. We use the NATO designations. As a general rule, the missiles with long-range trajectories can throw their RVs a maximum height of 500 to 800 miles above the Earth. RVs on IRBM trajectories reach heights of only 200 or 300 miles and reach their targets in somewhat less time.

Operational Land-Based Ballistic Missiles

SS-4

An older single-stage liquid-fuel IRBM, the SS-4 can throw a single nuclear warhead a distance of 1,200 miles. Slightly over 60 feet long, the SS-4 is quite large for its throw weight. Like most liquid-fuel warbirds, it does not boast high acceleration; and with its huge, thin-walled propellant tanks it would provide a rather stately, vulnerable target during its boost phase. Roughly 230 of these missiles have been deployed for years at fixed sites, some near the Chinese border and some, West of the Urals, aimed at targets in Western Europe.

SS-5

An older single-stage liquid-fuel IRBM, the SS-5 is outmoded and, like the SS-4, is being replaced by the formidable new SS-20. It is massive, over 70 feet in length, and therefore lacks mobility. It has been deployed for years at fixed sites near the Western borders of the Soviet Union. It can throw a single nuclear RV about 2,500 miles against European targets. The SS-5 was evidently never deployed in large numbers.

SS-11

A more sophisticated liquid-fuel warbird, the SS-11 has three stages which give it a range of 6,500 miles, easily into the ICBM category. It can throw only a single RV, however. Until recently, the Soviets had deployed more SS-11s, about 550 in all, at fixed sites than any other ballistic missile in their offensive arsenal.

SS-13

The SS-13 is the Soviet equivalent of our early Minuteman; a three-stage, solid-fuel ICBM with a 6,200 mile range throwing a single RV. About 60 of these missiles were deployed, then superseded by the SS-16. The SS-13 signaled the Soviet shift from liquid to solid fuels.

Solid fuels are not as efficient as the most energetic liquid fuels, but high-impulse liquid fuels cannot be easily stored in missiles for long periods. The fueling and checkout of a large liquid-fuel rocket is an hours-long process, but a solid-fuel rocket of almost any size can be stored for years if adequately protected against severe weather conditions, and then fired almost instantly. In addition, a typical liquid-fuel ICBM begins its mission accelerating rather slowly, at perhaps 0.5 'g'. A typical solid-fuel ICBM begins its acceleration at about four times that rate, i.e., 2 'g'. For military purposes the temperamental, complex liquid-fuel missiles cannot match the practicality of solids when instant readiness is the primary need. Our own Pershing, Minuteman, and Poseidon are all of the solid-fuel type.

SS-16

Like its predecessor the SS-13, the SS-16 is a three-stage, solid-fuel ICBM. It throws its single RV some 5,000 miles and is small enough to be considered mobile. By some accounts it is capable of throwing more than one RV. The Soviets have deployed them both in the North and the South.

SS-17

A two-stage, liquid-fuel ICBM, this warbird was one of the first to be armed with multiple, independently-targetable warheads. It can throw its 4 MIRV warheads 6,200 miles from widely-separated fixed sites in the Soviet Union. Some 150 of these missiles have been deployed as successors to the outmoded SS-11.

SS-18

A two-stage, liquid-fuel ICBM, the SS-18 must be considered a potential first-strike weapon. With its relatively low acceleration, it must continue on boost phase for roughly 300 seconds, allowing our defensive systems some 250 seconds between detection and "burnout", the end of boost phase. If aimed at targets near maximum range, the missile will reach burnout at a height of some 160 miles above the Earth, still climbing. Although very unwieldy—about 100 feet long and ten feet in diameter—the SS-18 boasts a range of 6,800 miles from fixed sites deep in Central Asia, and can loft its 8 or 10 MIRVs with very high accuracy. Our current figures for these missiles place their number at around 310.

SS-19

A more advanced version of the SS-11, this liquid-fuel ICBM has a much greater throw weight which permits as many as six MIRVs as payload.

SS-20

This two-stage, solid-fueled IRBM has a range of some 3,100 miles and can throw 3 MIRVs with very high accuracy. Its great advantages lie in its high acceleration, high mobility, and readiness to fire on short notice. Because the SS-20 propulsion system comprises two stages of the larger, three-stage SS-16, it could be converted to the larger warbird very easily. Since it uses solid fuel, the boost phase is short; our defensive sensors have relatively little time for detection and tracking during boost phase. Only 36 feet high, five and a half feet in diameter, it is transported on a mobile, self-propelled launcher which, analysts suspect, may carry two SS-20s for quick redeployment and quick reloading. This warbird will replace earlier SS-4 and SS-5 missiles. Deployment began in 1977.

The Soviet name for the SS-20 is the Pioneer. Between 300 and 400 of the new missiles are presently deployed, most of them West of the Urals within range of Western Europe. Some are positioned North of China. They can, of course, be repositioned anywhere the Red Army can take them.

The SS-20 is of very great concern to our Allies and, therefore, to us. According to SALT II criteria, its 3,100 mile range is—barely—beneath what would qualify the SS-20 as a strategic weapon, even though it can hurl its MIRVs from within the Soviet Union to targets in Western Europe and Japan. While the larger SS-16 is production-limited by SALT agreements, the Soviets could very quickly convert their SS-20s (which are not production-limited) to the larger weapon. It is the potency of the SS-20, a strategic nuclear weapon by all but SALT II criteria, that provoked Western plans to deploy the new Pershing II and cruise missiles in Europe (see Chapter 4).

Operational Sea-Launched Ballistic Missiles

In contrast to our early decision in the 1950s in favor of solid-fuel SLBMs, the Soviets first chose to develop liquid-fuel warbirds for sea launch. The complexity of liquid-fuel rockets makes them unsuitable for an SLBM role and, with their later designs, the Soviets have developed very potent solid-fuel SLBMs. The accuracy of a SLBM is likely to suffer from the fact that at sea a launching vessel's own position cannot be as precisely known as is a point on land.

SS-N-6

The Soviet counterpart of our early submarine-launched Polaris SLBM, this single-stage liquid-fuel missile has a range variously reported as 1,300 to 1,900 miles. The SS-N-6 carries 2 RVs; about 470 of them have been deployed on 'Y' class Soviet nuclear-powered submarines. A 'Y', or (ironically) 'Yankee', class Soviet sub can carry 16 missiles.

SS-N-8

This two-stage, liquid-fuel SLBM throws only one RV, but has an ICBM's range: 4,800 miles. Nearly 300 SS-N-8s have gone to sea with 'Delta-I' Class Soviet nuclear subs.

SS-N-17

This is the first solid-fuel Soviet SLBM, a two-stage missile with 2,400-mile range and a post-boost vehicle (PVB). A PVB has its own small steering rockets so that, after separation from the parent missile, the RV can be given final corrections for improved accuracy. Thus the SS-N-17 could probably be MIRVed, but is usually listed as throwing only one RV. Apparently only a dozen of these missiles were deployed.

SS-N-18

A later type of two-stage, liquid-fuel SLBM, this missile can throw 3 MIRVs about 4,000 miles. About 160 SS-N-18s have been deployed.

SS-NX-20

A very recent addition, this is a three-stage, solid-fuel SLBM which can throw 12 MIRVs about 5,100 miles. Its boost phase lasts perhaps 110 seconds, so our sensors would have around 60 seconds for tracking during boost phase. At burnout it may be some 50 miles above the Earth. For a SLBM it is massive; about fifty feet long and eight feet in diameter. As of September, 1983, only about 20 of these potent warbirds had been deployed. The SS-NX-20 is the Soviet counterpart to our long-range SLBMs.

ICBMS In Development

At least two land-based Soviet warbirds are in advanced development and may be deployed at any time. The PL-5 is a three-stage, solid-fuel ICBM which probably throws 3 MIRVs and may have a range of over 6,000 miles. The SS-X-24 is also a three-stage solid fuel ICBM and appears to be still more potent, probably with 10 MIRVs and a range between 8,500 and 9,000 miles.

Our information is, of course, sketchy on some details of the secret Soviet warbirds. In the past, however, U.S. Intelligence sources proved disconcertingly accurate. In a SALT meeting, one Soviet military negotiator asked U.S. officials not to divulge so much in the presence of Soviet civilians.

We will risk a speculation as to further developments in the Soviet arsenal. The latest of their missiles have high throw weight. If the U.S. deployed GBMD lasers, the Soviets might, by reducing the number of RVs in their payloads, be able to "harden" their missiles against a modest laser attack. The hardening would probably be shielding material to resist an HEL for longer periods—say, up to a second or so. Note well that a reduction in the number of RVs per missile is equivalent to a reduction in the number of missiles deployed, itself a goal devoutly to be wished for.

Antisatellite Warbirds

In 1977 the Soviets began testing a first-generation killer satellite against their own target satellites. That system is now almost fully operational. In early tests, the Soviet killer satellite, which boosted to orbit by modified ICBM, evidently needed one or two full orbits to stabilize its path for a subsequent kill. More recently the antisatellite ASCAT has made direct-ascent kills, i.e., it required less than one complete orbit to achieve its kill. In a typical intercept, the killer maneuvers into close proximity to a target and then explodes, blasting it with shrapnel or slugs. This system had undergone a score of tests by 1981. Placed atop a new D-I "Proton" booster, this ASAT might even have the capability to attack our satellites in geosynchronous orbit over 22,000 miles from Earth.

Between 1964 and 1975, the U.S. had a primitive operational ASAT system based on Johnston Island in the Pacific. Boosted into trajectory by a Thor booster but incapable of achieving orbital speed, the ASAT payload was timed to ascend to close proximity to its orbiting target. As the target satellite sped past, the ASAT's nuclear warhead was detonated by a signal from the ground. This system had several limitations and was dismantled nearly a decade ago.

A new, non-nuclear ASAT system is now in development by the U.S. Launched from an F-15 interceptor aircraft, a two-stage solid-fuel rocket follows a ballistic trajectory, in a manner conceptually like our earlier system. But the ASAT contains a super-cooled IR sensor which provides homing commands to the payload. Steering with small rockets, the entire homing ASAT collides with its target. This kinetic energy kill is very effective; while the target satellite must be moving some five miles per second, the ASAT vehicle itself has virtually no *orbital* velocity. A collision with many kilograms at five miles per second would destroy a battle tank! As of this writing House

Democrats of the left have very nearly succeeded in sending this program into limbo.

While the U.S. ASAT warbirds are suborbital, the Soviet ASAT is a fully-developed and tested orbiting killer satellite. Soviet technology in this area is disconcertingly ahead of ours.

Another area in which the Soviets appear to be far ahead, at least in operational hardware, is beam weapons, including continuous-wave high energy lasers (HEL). The Soviet HEL system at Sary Shagan may be the source of some troubling occurrences of the past, as for example the time when our IR satellites were blinded. The official explanation of "gas fires in Siberia" has not been universally accepted. In any event, the Sary Shagan installation is probably now capable of blinding our IR sensors all the way out to synchronous orbits. We suspect that the system is capable of more serious damage to satellites in lower orbits.

The Soviets have for some time engaged vigorously in high energy beam research, including use of nuclear-pumped beam weapons. While their ultimate goal is probably ICBM interception—the Soviets have always believed governments have a duty to protect their nations from hostile weapons— the immediate use would be against satellites.

The U.S. has invested heavily in military space assets, and must find some means of countering ASAT threats. One possibility, active defense of satellites, is fraught with problems, since it involves shooting at approaching objects even in time of peace. IBM Fellow Richard Garwin often points out that "space mines" could destroy any satellite at any time. He therefore proposes a comprehensive arms control agreement banning the testing, deployment, and use of ASAT weapons as the only means to defend U.S. military satellites. He is joined in this argument by many others; their arguments are examined in the next chapter.

Another possibility would be to place attack-warning sensors on new satellites, so that a satellite damaged by beams or kinetic energy weapons may be able to report the event. This would guard against "sneak attacks," but such sensors are unlikely to be able to distinguish between genuine attacks and freak accidents. Obviously, if several U.S. satellites experience "unusual accidents," the interpretation is clear, although what we might do in such instances is not so obvious. The Department of State has officially accused the Soviet Union of violating the Hague and Geneva Conventions against chemical weapons, but so far we have done nothing beyond making the accusation. The problem of what to do when arms control agreements fail has never been extensively studied, even by those who advocate such agreements as the major means for increasing U.S. national security.

Another result of ASAT technology will be that both sides begin to position some of their space assets far beyond geosynchronous orbit. If placed in an orbit of, say, 100,000 miles, a C^3I satellite would be far enough away that nothing but a beam weapon could reach it in several hours. By that time it would be clear that a distant satellite was due for a close encounter of an unpleasant kind.

However, the "tripwire" value of warning systems cannot be exaggerated. One of the grave strategic problems facing U.S. military planners is the short warning times we would have in the event of a nuclear strike. As warning times grow shorter, the pressure to launch the ICBM force and thus "use them before we lose them" becomes great during times of high international tension. This is the very definition of an unstable situation. Increased warning times inevitably aid the defender, not the aggressor, and by lowering the value of a first strike, increase strategic stability.

The best long-term solution to ASAT is probably hardening. Some electronic hardening is already designed into new satellite systems: surrounding them with a screen (known as a Faraday cage) can greatly aid in protecting their electronics from electromagnetic pulse (EMP) effects. Real hardening, though, requires mass, and lots of it. For example: a shell system, consisting of alternate layers of hard and soft-absorptive materials (known irreverently among strategic analysts as "concrete" and "shaving cream") will protect against kinetic energy weapons.

Although the shells need be really thick only on the leading edge, the requirements for hardening mass can grow rapidly, especially since the ideal case we would want the satellite to be invulnerable to anything except a nuclear weapon. Detonation of a nuclear weapon in proximity to a U.S. defensive satellite would be an unambiguous warning.

Hardening against beam weapons also requires mass: the mass is used as a heat sink to absorb, distribute, and re-radiate at leisure the beam energies directed against the satellite.

Although early satellites would carry hardening material from Earth, the mass requirements for hardening grow rapidly as the defense force becomes more effective. We will need space materials; in particular, we will need lunar soil, "green cheese," as it is called. Green cheese is not cheap: the first ton delivered into orbit could cost as much as $20 billion. However, once the first batch is delivered, the "marginal cost" plummets rapidly.

(Many analysts seem to confuse "marginal cost" and "average cost." They shouldn't. The average cost of, say, a ton of green cheese in Earth orbit is simply the total cost of the program divided by the number of tons delivered. That cost will remain high until a lot of tons are delivered. The marginal cost is the cost of the *next* ton. Since you have already paid the R&D costs as well as the cost of the initial Lunar installation, the *marginal cost* of a ton of lunar material in Earth orbit can be surprisingly low.)

There are obvious secondary benefits to the use of extra-terrestrial materials for satellite hardening; indeed, the scientific and economic benefits from the expanded space program, including a return to the Moon, could dwarf the costs of the defense systems.

The United States has *always* recovered more than the costs of space research. (Space enthusiasts claim returns of up to 14-for-1 over costs; critics say the space program returns "only" two-for-one, and a few say it "only" pays for itself. No serious analyst believes it does less than that.) Moreover, as space exploitation continues, there is greater economic wealth, in both energy and material, for the entire world. Some believe that a wealthy world is a world of fewer tensions and thus less likely to require—or use!—strategic weapons.

Protecting satellites, although worthwhile, is a costly and difficult undertaking. Since both the U.S. and the U.S.S.R. have ASAT capabilities, some analysts (who generally oppose an expanded space program on other grounds) affect to despair of sufficient satellite protection, and so turn to arms control agreements as the only way to preserve valuable U.S. space asssets. Some of these negotiations, and their pitfalls, are described in the next chapter.

CHAPTER FOUR

Wargames And Treaty Games

Richard L. Garwin and John Pike, "Space Weapons," Bulletin of the Atomic Scientists, May, 1984, p. 25.

"Our conclusion, based upon many years of involvement with strategic offensive weapons, strategic defenses and military space systems, is that an effective ban on anti-satellite activities and on weapons in space would best serve the national security interests of the United States. Furthermore, an effective ban is feasible and can be negotiated quickly."

In its June, 1984 annual meeting in New York the American Association for the Advancement of Science (AAAS, usually called "triple ay ess") dedicated several panels to problems of strategic weapons. The nearly unanimous conclusion of these panels is reflected in the statement by Richard Garwin and John Pike quoted at the opening of this chapter. This was reported in *The New York Times* and other papers as endorsement by "nearly all scientists" of the Garwin-Pike position.

There was significant, although unreported, opposition to the Garwin-Pike position. Robert Jastrow, former NASA space scientist and now a professor at Dartmouth, dismissed Garwin's analysis as hopelessly biased, and his arguments as "twaddle, too silly to pay attention to." Arthur Kantrowitz, often called "the father of the high energy laser," was less colorful, but equally unwilling to agree to Garwin's arguments. Kantrowitz was present at the meeting, but not invited to participate on the strategic analysis panels; his presentation was an address to the youth meeting on the nature of science.

The *Times* failed to note that with few exceptions all of the participants in the AAAS panels had been previously associated with Garwin and Pike or their organizations, and were known to reject the President's Strategic Defense Initiative; most, including Garwin and Pike, routinely use derisive phrases like "Star Wars" to refer to the SDI, and some refer to the President as "Darth Vader." Far from an objective discussion of issues, the AAAS panels were stacked in advance, and their conclusions were as inevitable as they were tendentious.

Richard Garwin, for example, was invited to appear on *all* of the strategic analysis panels, and in the press conferences as well; Dr. Jastrow was allowed to speak on one panel only; he was out-numbered on that one.

Oddly, no member of this Council was asked to participate on any of the strategy analysis panels, this despite the fact that the Council Chairman and several of its members have routinely been involved in AAAS activities, and once sponsored a session that drew the largest attendance in AAAS history. The 1984 AAAS meeting can hardly be called objective, and the organization of their treatment of what is, after all, the most important strategic question of the decade, does not reflect credit on the organized scientific community. Opponents of the Garwin-Pike position will have little choice but to call into question the competence of "scientific" organizations to comment on important matters of science: when the AAAS and other "scientific" organizations totally ignore a large number of scientists (including Dr. George A. Keyworth, science advisor to the President), then one must doubt their ability, as organizations, to contribute to strategic debate.

The AAAS panels could not have been stacked by "accident." Richard Garwin has for some years rejected every new U.S. weapon system proposed by the Administration in favor of some scheme of his own. Two years ago at a AAAS meeting Garwin advocated a new U.S. missile system based on 25 to 50 tiny mini-submarines each sub to carry five crewmen and two single-warhead, inaccurate "city buster" missiles. The operational absurdity of this proposal did not deter Garwin from arguing strenuously for it, nor did it prevent many of his fellow "concerned scientists" from advocating it in place of both the B-1 Bomber and the MX Missile. One is tempted to wonder if Dr. Garwin understands the laws of logic.

James Pike, meanwhile, is the associate director for space policy at the Federation of American Scientists. The FAS report on SDI was one of the first to point out that the Soviet Union could counter laser defense weapons "simply" by spinning the booster. They did not observe that this would be tantamount to self-disarmament, since all the boosters would have to be replaced.

It is simply not true—and they *know* it is not true—that "no one in the scientific community supports the President's "Star Wars proposal," as claimed by Garwin, Pike, and their various concerned and federated supporters, just as it is simply untrue—and again they know it—that no one in the scientific community favors the new space station. The science community is much broader than the coterie dominated by Carl Sagan and Richard Garwin.

The Garwin-Pike article cited purports to "prove" that ICBM interception is impossible. Part of their "proof," presented at the AAAS meeting, consists of ridiculing the idea of using "faster than light weapons" as impossible. Of course such weapons *are* impossible (or at any rate there is now no respectable physical theory that would allow them); nor has anyone who is sane ever advocated them.

Another straw man which superficial critics knock apart are kinetic energy weapons which pop up from silos in the U.S. and travel 6,000 miles through space to accomplish boost-phase intercepts of Soviet ICBMs. It is easy to prove that such weapons are virtually impossible, and some analysts gleefully do so. They do not seem to have noticed that no one ever proposed such weapons. The quality of their other analyses can be seen from the following:

Garwin and Pike assume that the Soviet Union has "adapted" their strategic offensive force. Since, in their words, "the boost phase of an adapted offensive force lasts a short time (40–100 seconds), and defensive systems stationary with respect to the likely launch areas are either based on the Earth, in its atmosphere or in GEO (in any case 10,000 to 40,000 kilometers from the launch). It is thus not possible to attack with rocket-propelled defenses, unless the rockets can be fired *before* ICBM or SLBM launch, in confidence that the offensive weapons will be launched only to be destroyed!" (Italics and exclamation point in original.)

They continue, "proving" that no other means for ICBM interception are possible; indeed, that the very idea is silly, and that anyone who could advocate such systems must be deranged. A complete refutation of their breathlessly written papers would require a larger work than this, and would be filled with tedious mathematics. Suffice it to say that such analysis can be done, and scientists with impeccable credentials—including Dr. George A. Keyworth, Jr., Science Advisor to the President, as well as members of this Council—have done that work.

The "concerned scientists'" words and numbers are impressive, and *given their assumptions*, their conclusions may logically follow; but the assumptions are entirely flawed. They and their union of concerned assistants are apparently unaware of even the most elementary papers, such as Maxwell Hunter's "Halloween Paper" which is reprinted in this book as an appendix. (Other technical papers are included in the full Council report available from the L-5 Society.)

Of course we do not say that there is no place for diplomacy, negotiation, and arms control in U.S. defense policy; but any such agreements must be based on *facts*, not on fanciful and misleading analyses by professional "arms controllers" bent on proving that their specialty is more important to U.S. security than is technology. The United States has an impressive record of technological achievements. Our track record in psychology and diplomacy is not very good. We should trust our lives and freedom to our strengths, not to our weaknesses.

War Games And Strategic Analysis

Far from being a cynical and insensitive self indulgence, the study of wars as if they were games is necessary for our survival. "Games", after all, are a series of "IF . . . THEN . . ." statements, with precisely defined rules. So are the "laws of science." Scientists call such systems of "IF . . . THEN . . ." statements "models". Many educators (including several members of the Council) believe that the study of games can be a valuable way to learn more about the nature of science and technology. In any event, since all computer simulations must be based on precise rules, they are technically "games".

The Theory of Games, largely developed by John von Neumann ("father of the modern computer") to analyze economic competitions, is a method for studying games by analysis of their strategic choices and payoffs. Game theory is often used for analysis of military situations; as Clausewitz observes, wars and treaties are special aspects of political/economic competition.

War is the most savage aspect of gaming, while a

treaty establishes agreements as to the rules of competition so that war can be avoided or, at least, mitigated. It should not surprise anyone that, when the players establish rules for their own games, the rules agreement—the process of treaty negotiation—itself becomes a serious game.

In most competitive games, such as, say, tennis, a player wins by the same score as his opponent loses. It means the same thing to say that Player A wins as to say Player B loses by that same margin. Whatever the final score, the sum of the winner's plus points and the loser's minus points is zero. That, in the jargon of game theorists, is a "zero-sum game". But treaty-making need not be a zero-sum game; if both sides profit by a rule, to some degree the treaty becomes a "non-zero-sum game". Similarly, both sides might lose. The treaty might be the source of a catastrophic war, for example. The shift from MAD to Assured Survival can be a non-zero-sum game because both sides can profit enormously by that shift. Citizens of every country can profit as soon as they begin to receive a measure of protection they cannot have with MAD; and in the long term, they receive the benefits of peaceful applications of technology.

The primary purpose of treaties is to avoid conflict. If you don't believe that, consider how often the abrogation or violation of one leads to violence. Treaties and other international agreements must be based in large part on a thorough understanding of the art and science of warfare; why wars happen; how they are fought; who will probably win . . . if anyone. Therefore, we must study war scenarios—in Kahn's phrase we must "think about the unthinkable"—if our treaties are to help us to avoid war. These analyses come in different flavors: some analyze a particular aspect of warfare. Dr. Stefan Possony's appended paper, "Time Factors in ICBM Defense," is a brief example of this kind of analysis. Other aspects studied in isolation and combination by members of the Citizens Advisory Council on National Space Policy include strategic analysis, orbital mechanics, synergism effect and absorption of new technology (facets of system analysis), and battle management. While some scenarios direct engagements of pre-defined forces, the goal of others may be to determine a system capable of prevailing against a given enemy force. The following is an example of such a force-counterforce analysis.

A Space Based Defense Scenario

Council members Drs. Colin Mick, Stefan Possony and Horst Salzwedel have specified a complete set of components sufficient to deploy and support a candidate GBMD system. Their system uses both space-based and ground-based components and is broadly distributed both in space and time; initial operational capability (10C), the date when a component can begin to be deployed, ranges for various elements from the very near future to the late 1990s. Note well: even the very first elements would add significantly to our security.

The overall system has the following components:

- A space-based detection and tracking system
- Space-based weapons for boost-phase intercept
- Space and ground systems for coast-phase intercept
- Ground-based systems for terminal-phase intercept
- Production and service centers for all weapons
- Space- and ground-based command and operations centers
- Transportation systems.

We would like to emphasize that all elements work together and depend on each other for maximum effectiveness. When this system or one like it is fully deployed, ICBMS will no longer be the most important element of military strategy.

The space-based detection and tracking system uses electromagnetic sensors and **TEAL RUBY** laser radar to detect missle launches and to track missiles throughout their flights.

Many candidates space-based weapons systems for

boost-phase intercept have been briefly described in this book. They ranged from HELS and Particle beams, missiles, to electromagnetic shock (to destroy guidance electronics).

Space- and ground-based delivery components for coast-phase ballistic intercept include space-based beam weapons and missiles launched from both spacecraft, and from high-flying aircraft (land and carrier-based). We emphasize again that detection and tracking systems for this phase—and this phase only—require further R&D for initial operating capability.

Ground-based systems for terminal-phase intercept employ directed energy weapons, including particle beams, and hypervelocity missiles launched from the ground as well as by aircraft.

Production, service, and repair facilities for all weapons include ground-based production centers; centralized, space-based repair stations; and remote (teleoperator and robotics) systems for servicing space-based devices.

Space-based command and operations centers are located in one or more polar-orbiting space stations, and/or a station in geosynchronous orbit, which house the military command and AI (artificial intelligence) support systems.

The transportation system consists of three basic elements: a launch system to move components into orbit; a launch system to transport personnel between satellites and Earth; orbital transport systems to move assets, including personnel, wherever necessary in orbit.

All of the systems together must guarantee the GBMD's operation before, during, and after attack. Full operational capability demands that the system perform under the most harrowing of conditions, and that elements can be readily serviced or replaced. It demands that the system be maintainable by field personnel including, perhaps, some in space, without immediate access to high-ranking scientists. The required differences are as similar and as great as those for maintaining a Formula One Ferrari versus those for a military Jeep. The Mick/Possony/Salzwedel model dramatizes the differences between a prototype device and an operational military device. Scenarios of this sort explain why operational systems are so costly. Military strategists must have high confidence that their systems are reliable; few things could be more destabilizing to strategists than operational systems that are not dependable on short notice. The shift from liquid to solid fuels in ballistic missiles was a case in point.

The Stability Issue

Some wargaming might be better called "peace-gaming," because it intentionally focuses on weapons international relations that the analysts believe tend to stabilize. All sides are wise to avoid more destabilizing weapons, i.e., those which provoke a preemptive attack because if war starts, everybody loses.

Deterrence is therefore very much a non-zero-sum game. A zero-sum game is one both sides want to win, and you can't afford to lose. In non-zero-sum games, everybody might lose to varying degrees, but it is also possible for everyone to win. Everybody would lose if nuclear war occurs—and not just when it starts. However, if nuclear war is deterred, then everybody wins, including the non-players. If we succeed with our strategy of deterrence, we are both winning for us and for the USSR population. If both sides get ABM defenses, then both sides still win.

A GBMD system's last name is 'defense', and to lessen provocation it must be as purely defensive as possible. Officials can no longer plausibly label an obviously offensive weapon as *de*fensive. There is more leeway in the case of a primarily defensive system which could take an offensive role, and systems analysis can sometimes reveal ways in which such a weapon can be verifiably kept in its defensive role without significantly diminishing its effectiveness in that role.

We must design a system capable of defeating a first strike; we must maintain a policy that involves some secrecy and some openness. (An opponent should obtain some significant information, yet not too much of it.) As Dr. Arthur Kantrowitz points out, whatever stability MAD has given has depended powerfully on the information we have gotten on Soviet developments from our observation satellites. Without this knowledge, MAD would be completely unstable in the face of self-excited rumor. Dr. Kantrowitz is fond of Madriaga's pithy dictum that "Nations don't distrust each other because they are armed; they are armed because they distrust each other."

While some secrecy is often vital, military secrecy has often been abused on all sides: in interservice rivalry; for partisan politics; to conceal official blunders; to conceal abuses of govern ment power. The strength of open societies is that openness reveals corruption, and short-term secrecy cannot long conceal corruption. We suggest that, in the process of erecting GBMD systems, all sides will profit from some deliberate openness, because only then can all sides gain stabilizing assurance that new defenses are not simply masked offenses.

We must also design against the most insidious of destabilizing events, war by mistake; conflict which Pulitzer-winner Thomas Powers has described as "... something darker and less predictable, something which happens to us without reason or purpose." A global ballistic missile defense system holds great hope for erasing the nightmare of a strangelovian accidental war, the isolated, perhaps accidental, launches of nuclear missiles. This is especially crucial now that we no longer have weeks or days in which to make decisions on a response. Until such a system is in place the US, the USSR, and the entire world are at the mercy of the vagaries of a launch-on-warning posture, on which more later.

In August of 1945, President Truman could openly state that the U.S. would continue to drop atomic bombs on Japan every few days until they surrendered. (Incidentally, he was bluffing. The U.S. had one unassembled bomb which could have been delivered within a few weeks.) The Japanese, under the impression that they had a deadline measured in days, surrendered a day later.

In 1962, President Kennedy had several days available for diplomatic maneuvering before making a final decision about attacking Soviet missiles in Cuba. Though we and the Soviets had a limited capacity for launching nuclear-tipped missiles, the brunt of nuclear assault at the time would have been carried by strategic bombers, which could be called back hours after takeoff.

Today, one of the worst aspects of nuclear strategy is that there is no time for diplomacy; minutes after the launch decision, there is no pulling back. But a nation capable of intercepting ICBMs in flight would not be subject to current restraints. It could afford to wait, to assess. If the response was to an "unauthorized" partial strike both sides, indeed *everyone*, would profit from GBMD because, suffering less or no damage, the defender would not be obliged to retaliate, or at worst would not be obliged to retaliate to the same degree.

The "accidental war" issue is often misunderstood. No volley of missiles can ever be launched without a command, and a command for an attack by the entire force cannot be mounted by an isolated rebellious general—who, for that matter, would first shoot at his enemies at home.

One or two missiles might be launched by accident. It does not matter whether the accident has technological, provocatory, or mutinous roots. Its essence is that only a minimum number of missiles is involved, and all other indicators of a real attack are missing. Those one or two missiles may kill many people, of course; and will face the President or other surviving decision maker with grave problems. If a major US city were destroyed, for example, accident or not the

American response would have to be designed to prevent a recurrence of such an act. Strategic consequences may be unlikely, but it would be far better if the missiles had been shot down automatically by the ABM system.

Even if there is a deliberate attack, if the defender need not retaliate, he will not lose his offensive strength. On the other hand, if the attack takes place and is intercepted, the attacker will lose most of his offensive strength, and will therefore be more or less disarmed. The defender, unhurt, becomes the leading power. Thus, anti-missile defenses upgrade deterrence by a whole dimension: given such defenses, attack places victory in the defender's hands. The better the defenses, the less chance that war will take place, and the more stable the world.

The problem of accidental war and other partial strike scenarios would be greatly reduced by even a very limited deployment of space-based missile defenses. Certainly a limited deployment would not appear to opponents as anything approaching an invulnerable shield. The present Soviet killer satellites, for example, pose no invulnerable threat. Limited deployment also has the obvious economic advantage of lower cost. Thus strategic analysis suggests that even a limited GBMD system has very great stabilizing potential in reducing the likelihood of accidental war.

The analysis also suggests a lesser, and temporary, potential to increase the likelihood of deliberate war, if one country perceives that an opponent is about to erect a GBMD. If it believes that offensive war becomes a "now or never" choice, that country could choose the "now" option, presumably hoping against all odds that the choice is not suicidal. It seems overwhelmingly likely that the U.S. has chosen the "never" option, in view of evidence that the Soviets have already begun assembling components of a GBMD. We believe it is almost as likely that the Soviets will make the same rational choice. Their ungracious but sober response to U.S. plans for a manned space station bolsters our belief. While it would be possible to deploy GBMD weapons that could be used as weapons of mass destruction, and thus be seen as destabilizing, the far better (and stabilizing) choice is to deploy defensive systems that could not be used for mass destruction.

Opponents of Assured Survival often argue both ways: first, they say, BMD can't work, and will be so expensive that it will bankrupt us. Having said that, they then say that the threat of BMD will be so great that the Soviets, fearing that the system will be perfect, will instantly attack upon deployment of the first BMD elements.

These arguments are mutually contradictory and individually absurd. Leak-proof defense systems are impossible. With the best defenses we can construct, the casualties in a nuclear war would be horrifyingly high. No sane President will begin a nuclear war under the delusion that our defense systems will keep U.S. casualities to some "acceptable" level; no Soviet planner will believe that either we or the Soviets can deploy a leak-proof system. Far more likely than the Soviets launching a probable suicide strike is that they would accelerate work on their own ABM system.

A generation ago, advocates of MAD rejected GBMD because it could not be made leakproof. But there is an advantage in unpredictable but certain leakage; even the best GBMD would not tempt rational planners into a first strike. One the one hand they know their counterstrike force will always be able to inflict terrible though not annihiliating damage, and on the other even if we know a leakage rate, we cannot know in advance where the leakage will be (just as we can closely predict auto accidents, but cannot know which drivers will be injured, nor where the injuries will occur). Thus a planner contemplating attack on the U.S. cannot know which of his offensive weapons will penetrate, and which surviving U.S. targets will be our own offensive weapons. As this uncertainty of success increases, the incentive to attack decreases. This kind of uncertainty is highly stabilizing.

The same uncertainty applies to U.S. planners, of course. Further, point defenses and hardened silos make a GBMD system more effective in defending weapons than in defending cities. While we might be willing to accept the loss of, say, 25% of our Minutemen, no elected official would consider the loss of a single U.S. city as "acceptable." The U.S. would have essentially zero incentive to launch a preemptive strike even with a fully operational GBMD. We are admittedly less certain how the Soviets view their incentives, but that is surely no argument against *our* GBMD.

The bankruptcy of MAD is further illustrated by the fact that, given vulnerable offensive weapons and no GBMD, we might have no better warfighting strategy than "launch on warning". This is *not* a good strategy; it is far less stable than one employing GBMD. But if we were to fall back on MAD, we will inevitably be forced to adopt the launch-on-warning response, and to announce it. Given short warning times, the incentive to employ Automatic "War Games" computer decision structures is high.

The new currency of Assured Survival should have other stabilizing, strategic advantages; for example, when both sides have effective defenses against ballistic missiles, the value of those ballistic missiles is diminished. And once nations see them diminished in value (while remaining just as expensive), there will be much less incentive to add more of them, or even retain all of them.

At the very least, defensive systems greatly increase warning times, while also enormously complicating the attacker's war plan. Granting that space components of a BMD system may be vulnerable, they must still be removed; and attacks against the space elements of a BMD system must come *before* the launch of a massive first strike.

While we may not be able to harden BMD satellites to invulnerability (although, given lunar materials to use as heat sinks and radiation shielding they can be made very hard indeed), they can certainly be hardened sufficiently to require use of a nuclear weapon against them. Needless to say, nuclear attack on a U.S. BMD satellite would be an unambiguous act of war; after such an event there would be no possibility of a Soviet strike catching our country unawares.

In arms-control agreements, the U.S. should work toward a set of rules explicitly permitting defense-only systems, with inspection safeguards. We should negotiate methods for clear identification of accidental offensive events, which would allow both sides to develop virtually automatic defensive intercepts. This would place GBMD systems in an even more stabilizing role. We must not, however, wait for ratification of such agreements; even if the Soviets were not assembling GBMD components, we would still be wise to do so. Since the systems they are developing clearly are—to put it diplomatically—'readily adaptable' to a Soviet GBMD, we should be doubly motivated. For it is becoming clear that, in the GBMD issue, America has three possible futures.

In one of those futures, both the West and the Soviets erect weapons in space more or less concurrently. In the second, the U.S. obtains its space-based GBMD first. Historically, we have an excellent record of permitting others, even competitors, to obtain parity. In the third possible future, the Soviet Union obtains its space-based GBMD first. Historically, the Soviets have *never* willingly given up an advantage and, given a powerful military advantage in space, it would be utterly fatuous to expect them to do other than deny the U.S. free access to space as ruthlessly as they deny free commerce and passage to citizens of Eastern Europe.

It is worth repeating that the Soviets currently have the world's only operational space weapons, and are expanding broad efforts to achieve military dominance of near-Earth space. But they know that

U.S. technological advantages in microelectronics and our operational shuttle would, given the national will, permit us to regain parity in space. We can expect them, therefore, to press for treaties which deny us the option of countering their advantages with space-borne defenses of our own while they continue, somewhat hampered by the need for discretion, to develop theirs apace.

If there must be an arms race, any sane person must prefer a solely defensive one. Arms competition may or may not be inevitable among competing technological societies, but surely movements away from offensive competition are useful to all sides. Since no country has limitless funds for arms, a large, truly defensive commitment should curb offensive spending—a fact which may largely have escaped advocates of nuclear freeze movements. But through detailed study of wargames and treaty games, serious analysts of all political stripes have begun to concede that, in Assured Survival, we have a strategy that curbs offensive spending while making populations less vulnerable to war, deliberate or accidental.

PERTINENT TREATIES

It is all too common for parties to a treaty to violate that treaty; but in some cases, parties scrupulously observe a treaty that was never ratified. At present the U.S. and the Soviets are supposedly bound by two ratified treaties dealing with ballistic missile defense. Both parties abide by provisions of a third and more recent treaty, although it was not ratified by the U.S. Senate.

Outer Space Treaty

This agreement was ratified by the U.S., the Soviet Union, and and many other countries in 1967. The correct title for the agreement is too long for any headline: "The Treaty on Principles Governing the Activities of States in Exploration and Use of Outer Space, Including the Moon and Other Celestial Bodies."

Article IV of the Treaty applies to the conduct of military activities in space and is reproduced below in its entirety.

ARTICLE IV

States parties to the Treaty undertake not to place in orbit around the Earth any objects carrying nuclear weapons or any other kinds of weapons of mass destruction, install such weapons on celestial bodies, or station such weapons in outer space in any other manner.

The moon and other celestial bodies shall be used by all States Parties to the Treaty exclusively for peaceful purposes. The establishment of military bases, installations and fortifications, the testing of any type of weapons and the conduct of military maneuvers on celestial bodies shall be forbidden. The use of military personnel for scientific research or for any other peaceful purposes shall not be prohibited. The use of any equipment or facility necessary for peaceful exploration of the moon and other celestial bodies shall also not be prohibited.

The ban on placing nuclear weapons in orbit, on the moon and other celestial bodies, or otherwise stationing them in outer space, is quite explicit. The reference to weapons of "mass destruction" is generally understood to mean chemical, biological, or radiological agents capable of causing death to masses of people, or devastation to large areas of property. But the term "mass destruction" is not defined in the treaty, so it is subject to interpretation.

Conventional weapons such as explosives, projectiles, and missiles are not included in this ban. Beam weapons such as chemical lasers in the tens-of-megawatts range could not cause mass destruction and would not be banned by this treaty. A "pop-up" nuclear-driven X-ray laser seems admissible, also; its nuclear payload is not stationed in orbit any more than an SS-20's nuclear warhead is 'stationed' in its brief passage above the biosphere. It is intriguing to speculate on the changing of definitions when the Soviets complete their Cosmograds, cities in space. At some point in the populating of space, enough people will reside in an extraterrestrial habitat to make many conventional devices, at least potentially, weapons of "mass destruction."

Consider the American space station, Skylab, which fell out of orbit in 1979, scattering debris in a swath across the Indian Ocean and portions of Australia. The orbital velocity of Skylab gave it kinetic energy equivalent to about half a kiloton of TNT. Was Skylab a potential weapon, or at least an agent, of mass destruction? Boundaries of this kind blur when you focus on them.

Various schemes have surfaced for the development of a fractional orbital bombardment system (FOBS), which would achieve orbital velocity for a brief period—less than a complete orbit. The FOBS warhead would perform a propulsive maneuver and reenter before completing a full orbital revolution. Assuming that such a system carried weapons of mass destruction, it might be thought that a FOBS would be banned by the Outer Space Treaty; but it is not. Then-Secretary of Defense Robert McNamara made the interpretation that a FOBS is not banned, because it is not "officially" in orbit *until it has completed one full revolution around the Earth.*

There are precedents for conventional weapons in space, and for nuclear weapons that transit through space. The Soviet killer satellite is an example of the former; and the whole panoply of nuclear-tipped ballistic missiles comprises examples of the latter.

The Outer Space Treaty is under United Nations sponsorship. Many other nations signed it in addition to the U.S. and the Soviet Union. The treaty requires one-year notice by any nation of its withdrawal from the treaty, before that withdrawal takes effect.

ABM Treaty

The ABM treaty also has an official name: "The Treaty Between the United States of America and the Union of Soviet Socialist Republics on the Limitation of Anti-Ballistic Missile Systems." Signed and ratified in 1972, this agreement was amended in 1974 with a brief "Protocol." The ABM Treaty is often misquoted and misunderstood in discussions on proposed defensive systems, both space- and ground-based. The key to the treaty is the careful and limited definition of an ABM system, stated in Article II of the ABM Treaty. We reproduce it here below.

ARTICLE II

1. For the purpose of this Treaty an ABM system is a system to counter strategic ballistic missiles or their elements in flight trajectory, currently consisting of:

(a) ABM interceptor missiles, which are interceptor missiles constructed and deployed for an ABM role, or of a type tested in an ABM mode;

(b) ABM launchers, which are launchers constructed and deployed for launching ABM interceptor missiles; and

(c) ABM radars, which are radars constructed and deployed for an ABM role, or of a type tested in an ABM mode.

2. The ABM system components listed in Paragraph 1 of this Article include those which are:

(a) operational;
(b) under construction;
(c) undergoing testing;
(d) undergoing overhaul, repair or conversion; or
(e) mothballed.

This article explicitly limits the definition of an ABM system. To be addressed by the ABM Treaty, an ABM system must fit within particular technologies consisting of interceptor missiles, launchers, and radars. This is a crucial limitation of the treaty because it does not address many systems which can be used for defense against ballistic missiles.

In the same treaty, further articles limit the number and location of ABM components. Most often referenced is Article V.

ARTICLE V

1. Each Party undertakes not to develop, test, or deploy ABM systems or components which are sea-based, air-based, space-based, or mobile land-based.

2. Each Party undertakes not to develop, test, or deploy ABM launchers for launching more than one ABM interceptor missile at a time from each launcher, not to modify deployed launchers to provide them with such a capability, not to develop, test, or deploy automatic or semi-automatic or other similar systems for rapid reload of ABM launchers.

This article seems to prohibit ABMs based in space, air, sea, or mobile land launchers. Yet it prohibits *only those ABMs using the technology carefully outlined in Article II.* Does either country have a space-based system which could be used against ballistic missiles, but does not use interceptor missiles or radar technology? They are not limited by this Article.

However, a special Agreed Statement regarding other ABM technologies was appended to the ABM Treaty and initialed by the Heads of Delegations when the original treaty was signed in 1972. It was labeled 'D' .

AGREED STATEMENT D

In order to insure fulfillment of the obligation not to deploy ABM systems and their components except as provided in Article III of the Treaty, the Parties agree that in the event ABM systems based on other physical principles and including components capable of substituting for ABM interceptor missiles, ABM launchers, or ABM radars are created in the future, specific limitations on such systems and their components would be subject to discussion in accordance with Article XIII and agreement in accordance with Article XIV of the Treaty.

So Agreed Statement 'D' leaves room for amendments that would limit ABM systems using principles and components other than interceptor missiles, launchers, and radars. No such amendment has ever been made to the ABM Treaty, however. As it now stands, the ABM Treaty does not limit ballistic missile defense technologies other than interceptor missiles and launchers, and radar systems. Other technologies are unlimited both in number and in deployment location.

Article VI of the treaty is of particular interest because the Soviets have violated it.

ARTICLE VI

To enhance assurance of the effectiveness of the limitations on ABM systems and their components provided by the Treaty, each Party undertakes:

(a) not to give missiles, launchers, or radars, other than ABM interceptor missiles, ABM launchers, or ABM radars, capabilities to counter strategic ballistic missiles or their elements in flight trajectory, and not to test them in an ABM mode; and

(b) not to deploy in the future radars for early warning of strategic missile attack except at locations along the periphery of its national territory and oriented outward.

We shall have good reason to refer to Article VI later in this chapter when discussing treaty violations. The Soviet Union and the U.S. are the only

nations party to this treaty. Either nation may withdraw from the treaty by giving six months notice.

SALT II

This agreement is commonly called the SALT II
Treaty and Protocol, after the strategic arms limitation talks which led to the treaty. Officially it is
termed the "Treaty Between the United States of
America and the Union of Soviet Socialist Republics
on the Limitation of Strategic Offensive Arms." This
agreement was signed in 1979, but the United States
Senate refused to ratify it. Thus, the SALT II agreement is not officially in force. Leaders of both
countries, however, indicated that they would abide
by the treaty's limitations, which expire in 1985.
Had the treaty been ratified, either nation could have
withdrawn by giving the other nation six months
notice.

The section of the SALT II Treaty which directly
affects weapons systems is Article IX, subparagraph
C. We reproduce its text below.

ARTICLE IX

1. Each Party undertakes not to develop, test,
or deploy:

(c) systems for placing into Earth orbit nuclear weapons or any other kind of weapons of
mass destruction, including fractional orbital
missiles;

This article places somewhat stronger restrictions
on space weapons of mass destruction than does the
Outer Space Treaty. It specifically bans development
and testing of such systems, while the Outer Space
Treaty only bans actual placement of nuclear weapons themselves. The Salt II article also closes the
FOBS loophole of earlier treaties. As we have seen,
Secretary McNamara had argued in 1967 that fractional orbital weapons were exempted from the Outer
Space Treaty; but the language of SALT II is explicit
on the point, and bans FOBS.

Both sides seem to have generally adhered to the SALT II agreement, even though it remains unratified. This is not to say that SALT II is obeyed rigorously. For examples: the treaty permits each country one new missile type; all other ballistic missile development must be slight modifications of existing hardware. The modification limits are well-defined, requiring that the missile retain the same type of propellant (solid or liquid), the same number of stages, and maintain within five percent of the same throw weight, length, maximum diameter, and launch weight of the existing missile type. The agreement even specifies that the five percent modifications can be relaxed to ten percent, but only during the early test phase of the modified missile. These are subtle distinctions appreciated by designers during research and development programs.

As for U.S. compliance to SALT II, we have tested the one new missile type permitted by the treaty: MX, or Peacekeeper. We have considered development of another new ballistic missile, a relatively small solid-fuel design dubbed Midgetman. But Midgetman would be intended to replace Minuteman, though it would be significantly different from the existing missile. If we proceeded with Midgetman we would be in violation of SALT II, unless the U.S. obtained some amendment to the unratified agreement.

Proposed New Agreements

At different times, both the U.S. and the Soviet Union have proposed other treaties which would ban development, testing, and deployment of antisatellite systems. Such an agreement would be unlikely today, because verification would be next to impossible; an unverifiable ban between the U.S. and the USSR would be tantamount to a unilateral US freeze in whatever technologies were at issue. For that matter, the new U.S. antisatellite system is small enough to be launched from an F-15 fighter aircraft. It would be easy to hide the small interceptor missiles from inspection. They need no large silo or specialized launcher; only airfields, of which both nations have plenty.

The Soviets have recently proposed a total ban on weapons of any kind in outer space. Various scientists and others in the U.S. have supported such a ban. Total bans have little prospect for success for the same reason that antisatellite weapon treaties do not succeed: it is so unlikely that either side could verify compliance with such agreements, that enforcement of the treaty becomes almost impossible.

For the US to enter into such a treaty with the USSR would be very unwise because cheating is so easy and so potentially rewarding. A ban on outer space weapons would not prevent some nation—to be blunt, the Soviet Union—from secretly stockpiling weapons in space. Whenever it is ready to do so, it could perform a "breakout," destroying space assets of other nations so that the violator controls access to space. Other nations scrupulously observing the treaty would then be obliged to scramble to develop countermeasures if they could—or failing that to leave space in the hands of the nation that cheated.

If a treaty offers high potential for a breakout, then reasonable governments must, for their own protection, behave as though that treaty were indeed secretly being broken. The most likely outcome following a ban on space weapons would be for the U.S. to engage in preparing defensive countermeasures to suspected antisatellite weapons, probably with concurrent design work on our own antisatellite weapons. The only advantage to the ban would be to spare honest (or foolish?) nations the cost of building space weapon systems, but at the harrowing risk of a breakout by another nation.

The treaties on strategic missiles have largely worked because current offensive missiles and their associated components are huge and must be de-

ployed in large numbers. This factor permits monitoring from orbit, to eliminate (or at least minimize)
cheating.

Nor is the Soviet Union the only possible violator
of such a treaty. Several nations in addition to the
U.S. and the Soviet Union could develop and deploy
antisatellite systems using small solid-fuel boosters
with performance no more advanced that the venera-
ble U.S. Scout launch vehicle. Fifty launchers and
their interceptor payloads could destroy most spacecraft of any military value. Those boosters could be
openly produced and regularly launched on ordinary
scientific missions, then modified quickly for their
interceptor missions. If only because such breakout
scenarios are so plausible, a treaty that bans the
development of antisatellite weapons does not seem
likely in the future. If it were not for the current
vogue for arms control at almost any price, such a
possibility would not even bear discussion.

The most recent negotiations of note have been
the U.S.-Soviet talks regarding intermediate range
missiles. In 1977 the Soviets began massive deployment of their potent new SS-20 MIRV missiles near
the western borders of the Soviet Union. The SS-20s
cover Europe like a blanket; even Greenland isn't safe
from them. But thanks to Salt II's rather curious
definitions, the multiple-warhead SS-20 is not limited by treaty, and our European allies, rejecting
mute acceptance of this menace, requested new counterforce weapons from the U.S.

The U.S. response was to offer to deploy new Pershing IIs as replacement for older Pershing I missiles
which have been stationed in West Germany since
1969. The new Pershing II has a range of about 1,000
miles, considerably greater than its predecessor, and
is far more accurate. Even though the Pershing II
throws only one warhead per missile vs. three for the
SS-20, and its range is only a third of the SS-20, still
the new Pershing can reach targets in the western-
most part of the Soviet Union, and the Soviets cor-

rectly view the new missile as a real counterforce. The reason, however, that its continued deployment in the face of every kind of Soviet threat has driven them quite frantic is that the Pershing II is the first European-based weapon that threatens the Soviet's forward military command structure. The Pershing II is *very* accurate, accurate enough to be aimed at and hit a target as small, say, as a division headquarters building.

In addition to the Pershing II, the U.S. offered to base its new cruise missiles with its NATO partners. Our cruise missiles are small pilotless jet aircraft which, though flying at subsonic speed, can reach the Soviet Union from England. A difficult target at treetop altitude, the cruise missile can deliver its single 0.2 megaton warhead with pinpoint accuracy and is deployed from a mobile launcher. U.S. negotiators, by offering to call off deployment of our new weapons, hoped to persuade the Soviets to withdraw all their new SS-20s from positions that threatened Europe.

But this "Zero Option" (so named for its proposal to leave both sides with no new threats) would have required the Soviets to accept severe cuts in already-deployed weapons, while NATO forces would have only shelved plans to deploy new ones. To forego current overwhelming superiority for guaranteed future parity may be wise, but it is not the Soviet style. Further, the Soviets may be as proud of their SS-20 as we are of our space shuttles, and they have invested heavily in it. The Zero Option made no headway in Geneva. Some analysts suggest that the proposal's name was unfortunate, in that it seemed to imply an absolutist position with no room for maneuver or counterploy, rather than a preliminary negotiating stance. No one on the Council believed this was a significant factor, however.

The Soviet counterproposal started with a freeze followed by a gradual mutual reduction. Sometime near the turn of the century there would be no missiles or bombers. It sounded good until examined. The problem was that the Soviet offer counted ancient NATO weapons as equal to their own most potent weapons, and in general involved so much fraudulent arithmetic that it could hardly be taken seriously. They later made other offers, but none which gave NATO any reason to delay the advent of the new Pershings and cruise missiles. That deployment duly began in 1983 and continues as of this writing (July 1984). Perhaps the West will find the Soviets more amenable to symmetrical reductions.

The Soviets worked hard but fruitlessly to persuade West Germany against welcoming the new Pershings she had asked for when governed by the Social Democrats, hoping to divide NATO and create enough civil unrest that Chancellor Kohl might call off the German deployment. A Soviet propaganda victory would have yielded them a political victory in West Germany which, in turn, would have amounted to a Soviet victory in the arms negotiation game. Fortunately they were no more successful in this than in their earlier campaign to deny Kohl the Chancellorship.

Treaties are frequently delayed in this way, pending the outcomes of other serious gaming. At this writing, the Soviets have begun to deploy more missiles in Czechoslovakia and East Germany, and NATO continues to deploy counterweapons, while the treaty process languishes.

European Perspectives

Our European Allies who, after all, first asked for the U.S. weapons, have remained firmly committed to their counterforce option. France, with her determined go-it-alone stance, retains her own S-2 and S-3 counterforce ballistic missiles and, in addition, President Mitterand resolutely urged neighboring West Germans to stick with their original request for the new Pershings.

The Germans did just that. Despite demonstrations by vocal minorities, West Germans voted Chancellor Kohl his mandate to deploy the Pershings in 1983 and, because of the stalemate in Geneva, Pershing IIs are now deployed as requested. The German deployment had been the subject of much speculation by some other NATO countries, which regarded Germany's decision as vital.

Italy also remained firm in her commitment to accept NATO counterforce missiles. Even the Vatican agrees that the Soviet missile threat requires reciprocity; Italy's share of reciprocity includes over 100 Tomahawk cruise missiles.

Under Thatcher, England's stand was never in doubt (like France, England maintains her own nuclear deterrent as well). The Pershing II will not reach the Soviet Union from England (the SS-20, of course, will easily do the reverse); but the Tomahawk will fly the distance. England now has her cruise missiles.

If the proposed system could only defend the U.S., our Allies might reasonably view our GBMD as, at best, academic. But this is not the case; when fully deployed our GBMD will defend the world against nuclear missiles. American and Allied problems are both politically and technically synergistic; at a minimum, we should certainly investigate GBMD as a NATO effort. With European cooperation, even the early point defense phase could be installed on both continents, while space-based defenses such as Redding's layered defense scheme would involve Eastward-moving orbital platforms which could readily protect Western Europe from SS-20s. Given the many wartime scenarios that feature the U.S. and the USSR playing "nuclear football" in Europe while their respective homelands remain sacrosanct, NATO countries have an even starker motivation for GBVD than do we.

An SS-20 fired against a European target has, at most, only a few thousand miles to go; and this implies more stringent target-acquisition and tracking times against SS-20s. These heightened requirements mean that beam weapons (needing no built-in delays to accelerate kinetic-energy weapons) would probably be superior weapons from a European perspective. Allied cooperation in beam weapon development might be a strong aspect of a NATO missile defense.

It does not require a Nostradamus to predict the Soviet response to a European commitment in the GBMD arena. Our opponents have for some time enjoyed the creaks of internal stress within NATO, and do not relish the idea of revitalized relationships in the NATO fraternity. Because such a joint approach to a GBMD may be precisely what NATO needs, that approach would be set to martial music by Soviet propaganda composers. It will be interesting to see the many arguments Soviet analysts and American Federations of concerned leftists unearth to persuade Europeans *not* to participate in their own assured survival.

Treaty Violations

There are many ways to break a treaty: among them are violation by accident; violation of the treaty's intent while adhering to its language; and deliberate violation of both its language and its intent. We believe that a massive new Soviet radar installation in Siberia violates both the language and intent of the ABM Treaty. The new radar, coordinated with existing Soviet early warning radars, would provide accurate tracking for an ABM system nuclear battle-management. Its location is hundreds of miles inside Soviet borders and so violates Article VI (b) of the ABM Treaty, but still more important is the close proximity of that new radar to Soviet ICBM fields. The radar installation at Abalakova could readily direct ABM defenses for several crucial Soviet ICBM fields, notably SS-18 sites around nearby Novosibirsk.

The Soviets reply that the Abalakova radar is intended to track space objects, not ICBMs. Certainly it could do that. It is capacity, not intent, that is at issue. Whatever reasons the Soviets may give for

erecting the Abalakova radar, they cannot be unaware of its usefulness in ABM battle management.
And as for anyone who honestly believes that the
primary purpose of the installation is *not* battle
management, the authors invite him to contact us
about a business opportunity. We have this bridge . . .

Another apparent treaty violation involves rapid
reloading of the SH-08, a nuclear-tipped, point-defense
missile deployed as part of Moscow's legal ABM
system. We have observed tests at Sary Shagan in
which rapid reloading was tested within an SH-08
silo by two launches within two hours. This violates
Article V of the ABM treaty.

The upshot of these and other Soviet actions is
that they clearly no longer feel bound by SALT II,if
they ever did. Western observers report a new Soviet
solid-fuel ICBM called the PL-5, with a throw-weight
as of mid-1983 that may be twice as high as that of
the missile the Soviets claim it replaces, the SS-13.
The Soviets have already tested another new missile,
the one new missile type permitted by SALT II; if the
reports are correct, the PL-5 is different enough to be
a clear violation. The U.S., at this writing, is still
analyzing data from PL-5 test flights (which we moni-
tored from the Bering Sea and other positions). The
question of the PL-5 will be fully resolved in due
time.

Treaties pertaining to GBMD systems have given
the U.S. a decade of comparative relaxation at the
cost of current and future risk. The Soviets have used
that time to develop hardware that can be quickly
assembled as a layered ballistic missile defense
system—which, we repeat, the U.S. should have
begun long ago. A deployed Soviet GBMD, in the
absence of our own, would be an utter disaster. They
may be very close—within a year or two—to such a
breakout.

In assembling our GBMD system we must not abandon arms limitation agreements; on the contrary, we
might strive harder to obtain verifiable reductions in

offensive weapons. Not only do such agreements make a great deal of sense when compiled with GBMD, it seems likely that such a twofold improvement would be popular with advocates of various disarmament movements, particularly if the public gains more familiarity with the stabilizing effects of mutual GBMD systems by the superpowers. This improvement can be real, however, only if we move vigorously toward our GBMD. The cost of our system will be bearable. The cost of being denied free access to space, to say nothing of being put forever in a state of strategic inferiority bordering on hopelessness, would not be bearable.

Clemenceau once said that war is far too important a matter to be left to generals. It is also true that strategy is far too important to be left to scientists who have never made a scientific study of war, and academic planners who have a political program to implement. Most opponents of U.S. defensive weapons have never proposed any practical alternatives; they pin their faith on "negotiations," and their imagination never rises to a higher level. Negotiations and agreements can be important components of a strategy of survival, but they cannot themselves assure survival.

We believe the United States can do much better than mere survival. The nation or nations that take free people to space will assuredly do it with initial military spending—but spacefaring will repay economic benefits so huge as to guarantee world leadership within a generation.

CHAPTER FIVE

Exploring Our Frontiers

It is the historic role of government to provide roads to the new frontier, and to protect the early settlers.

—Fred Osborne.

During the Twentieth Century, several frontiers have followed the American West into oblivion. The African interior, Australia's Outback, the Polar regions, the Amazon West Basin—all are now regions known and charted well enough to support permanent settlements with modern comforts. Indeed, the plain fact is that when one speaks today of a new frontier, the listener is likely to think in terms intellectual, not physical.

The Council certainly does not undervalue the metaphorical frontiers of astronomy, or medicine, or metallurgy; without exploring the frontiers of science we would be ill-equipped to explore new physical frontiers. Alexander's legions used the best technology of their time to explore their frontiers— and sent back new discoveries to further Western science, in accord with Aristotle's request. Lewis and Clark, in their military exploration of the American West, carried such technical gadgetry as a collapsible boat and an airgun. (The airgun worked; the boat didn't.) They also collected a huge array of "natural science" specimens, many of them botanical, by Jefferson's order. There has always been a synergism between explorations of technological and physical frontiers. And military expeditions have always been among the most fruitful kinds of exploration. It is time that spacefaring nations, including the U.S. and the Soviets, all recognize and agree that physical and intellectual frontiers will be explored together beyond the Earth, and that it is perfectly acceptable for that exploration to begin with military spending. Space and celestial bodies compose a new frontier with both physical and scientific dimensions, and nations may explore it—are expected to do so—with military as well as civilian personnel.

The Issue Of Military/Space Exploration

This synergism between science and the military, during frontier explorations, is taken for granted by many analysts. We address it here because in some respected quarters, that traditional link has become an issue. A number of scientists in the West argue aloud that any military presence in space, even (or particularly) manned military presence, is dangerous and impedes the orderly investigation of space. Some of them continue to press for very great increases in scientific spending for space exploration while attempting to ensure that all of the exploration will remain "pure", i.e., free of the taint of military connection. They seem to believe, oddly, that planetary astronomy is more worthy of government funding than all other areas of science combined.

Some Council members, too, wish that a vigorous and purely scientific exploration of the high frontier were possible; but present evidence convinces us overwhelmingly that it simply isn't in the cards. We have already cited evidence that the Soviets, thanks to their orderly military/scientific advances on the high frontier, are near a "breakout" in which they could prevent passage of other nations into space for any purpose. And the Soviets continue to devote much more of their economic resources to military space developments than we do. Very few of their scientists seem reluctant to explore space in partnership with their military establishment. Still, a few in the West continue to search for some economic springboard by which we might vault into space as vigorously as the Soviets, without the initial aid (and the partial control it implies) of military spending.

The chances of our finding such a springboard are almost nil. The American taxpayer is unlikely to support a program costing billions annually unless that program offers some practical, visible improvement that is applied immediately, or almost immediately. Unfortunately, pure science and applied science do not always mesh. The taxpayer has every right to insist that a heavily-funded, tax-supported space exploration program will result in applied science; missile defense, better communications, better transportation, better medicine, better materials, a better biosphere; all to improve the quality of life. It is no coincidence that virtually all of these improvements are *exactly* what much of the military money is always spent on. American pre-eminence in international air transport sprang from the Douglas C-54 military transport which blazed the transoceanic air routes of the world beginning in World War II. The C-54 became the DC-4, the first postwar air transport. Today's wide-bodied airliners are the result of developments on USAF military transports. Military establishments need improved transportation, communication, medical science, materials, and in addition such things as new sources of materials—all of which have been passed on to the taxpayer in many such examples of military "seed money" later outstripped by commercial spending.

Well, then: if space promises commercial windfalls, why can't we obtain all the exploration funds from General Electric, General Mills, General Motors, and Private Enterprise? Because private enterprise is based on the profit motive, and its investors rarely sink billions *annually* into enterprises which cannot confidently be expected to show a dollar profit for a decade.

Numerous corporations are already risking investments in space research (as distinguished from government-funded efforts by corporation, which are not so risky), but they are responsive to their investors, too. They cannot, in the context of free enterprise, afford to commit billions to purely scientific space exploration. And even if some commercial firm wanted to commit a decade's profits to assets in space, it would surely balk at the investment if its assets could not be defended against outright piracy or covert sabotage. That defense has always depended on a military presence of some kind, under whatever label. We cannot expect any very large commercial *or* scientific exploration of our space frontiers that does not spring in large part from military spending.

For that matter, virtually all of our present scientific space assets were carried into space by boosters developed from military-funded technology. Had we refused the military/scientific connection a generation ago, we would still know nothing significant about minerals on the moon and Mars; nothing significant about atmospheres of moons in the Solar System. If we should now divorce space science from military connections, we might not impede military space developments much, but we would deal a crushing blow to peaceful American scientific space exploration.

Exploring and Occupying
Celestial Bodies

Since remotely-operated equipment cannot yet (if ever) perform all necessary construction maintenance and operations without humans to help, other space-faring nations must follow the Soviet lead with a greatly expanded presence in space. Two hazards facing such permanent presence in space are solar flares and hostile fire. Spacefarers know that the shielding of their spacecraft provides little protection against, say, an unpredictable solar flare. A permanent manned outpost, or settlement, beyond the Earth will require shielding, certainly for the humans and preferably for their equipment as well.

Shielding from solar radiation, and from attack, requires mass—a great deal of it. To supply it, we *could* simply launch many tons of prefabricated shielding material by shuttle to orbiting space outposts. But we would do so at enormous expense and with very little new knowledge to show for it. Furthermore, the thousandth ton would cost very nearly as much as the first. Another, and we believe better, option is to get it from the Moon, and later from the asteroids.

A Moon settlement, which would be needed to provide lunar mass for other locations, could be shielded very easily by lunar regolith—moondirt, as it were—processed with fabrication equipment brought from Earth and using abundant solar energy. We could, in fact, bore under the lunar surface to create pressure-tight interlinked tunnels or vast bubbles. Working in favorable conditions of low gravity there, we could then prefabricate lunar material as shielding for GBMD components and other vulnerable assets in Earth orbit. We can ship material from the Moon to Earth orbit with much less energy than would be required to ship that kilogram from "nearby" Earth which is not so near in terms of fuel because Earth's gravity is so much greater than that of the moon. We could also readily process Lunar regolith to supply provisions for further explorations and commerce. (see Chapter 7).

Our moon base would be very secure from direct attack since the available shielding would be, for all practical purposes, unlimited. Therefore, it would be logical to equip it to be a stand-by military communication and command center as well. Since light-speed communication is still almost instantaneous from the moon, a lunar base would be a highly secure location for strategic warning on Earth.

Those uncomfortable with the military connection should keep in mind that the lunar fort will doubtless give way in short order to the commercial lunar settlement. Any doubt that this military-to-civilian process is a thoroughly American tradition can be dispelled by searching, today, for the military commandants of Fort Lauderdale, Fort Smith, Fort Wayne, or Fort Worth.

Because of its nearness and its high potential as a secure base with vast raw resources, the moon is considered by some as the obvious candidate for early exploration and development. Some on the Council maintain that we cannot maintain an enduring space presence without a lunar settlement. Others suggest that the asteroids are a viable alternative.

One alternative would be to explore the Asteroid Belt, between the orbits of Mars and Jupiter, for attractive objects to be nudged into near-Earth orbit and then mined for materials and used as secure habitats. For the near term, fuel (and time) are the chief criteria, however, so initially at least we might retrieve some of the asteroids that move in orbits that approach the Earth. Numerous celestial bodies of this type have been identified and, with proper planning for minimum-energy missions, some could be "towed" to Earth orbit to be used as shielding. The energy requirements of this maneuver might actually be even less than to bring lunar shielding materials to near-Earth orbit. It would also be possible to achieve the final orbit even more cheaply, in fuel costs, by guiding the asteroid through the upper edges of the atmosphere for an aerobraking maneuver. Possible; but it would surely prove highly unpopular with the voting public, including many members of this Council. Several of these details are subject to the mission scientist's choice and the time frame in which they would occur. They do not appear to involve any technology beyond what we possess today. However, it should be kept firmly in mind that any such scheme to obtain asteroidal mass would be more exploratory than a mission to the moon. We *know* we can get to the Moon; anyone who chooses can stroke a piece of it by visiting the Smithsonian.

Not only would a lunar mine provide unlimited mass for hardening GBMD components and other space assets; such a base, especially if combined with asteroidal resources, will provide a solid staging area from which to explore the rest of the Solar system. Thanks to our preliminary explorations to date, we probably have enough experience to design expeditions to Mars and to some satellites of other planets. After all, a small moon with a predictable orbit and no atmosphere is something with which Council member Aldrin has considerable hands-on experience! A Mars mission would in turn provide a firm knowledge base for later missions to bodies with atmospheres that corrode our life-support equipment, and to planetoids subject to complex orbital variations. This time, America will be in space to stay.

Since our lunar base is intended to be permanent and later manned expeditions will last for years, we also need more expertise in life-support systems for extended periods. Permanently-manned space stations are a vital step in this process. Robots and remotely-operated (teleoperator) devices also have great potential for exploratory missions and, eventually, might be preferable to humans in some explorations. We have enough experience, in short, to predict some of the problems we will face in exploring the frontiers of the Solar System. Thus far, we have found no problems that could not be solved by a vigorous, long-standing commitment to exploration.

We repeat that every nation's initial explorations will probably involve military spending. Whatever our source of funds, we will cease to be a leading world power when we no longer have the ability or the will to explore the frontier of space. This is especially true since an avowed opponent *does* exhibit the ability and the will. Make no mistake; if we fail this test, History and the Soviets will allow no second thoughts.

Can we "mine" the atmospheres of Titan and Jupiter with ramscoop vehicles? Can Mars be terraformed? We must explore these largely unknown bodies before we can know the answers, but they may be among the most important answers in the future of the human race.

CHAPTER SIX

Peace and Assured Survival

We believe that if America moves to a strategy of assured survival then the effects of nuclear war would be very much mitigated. We believe, just as strongly, that assured survival will infinitely reduce the *chance* of such a war. Aside from assuring its existence, of what use is assured survival in a world at peace?

Because we will initiate the new strategy during peacetime, and because it is designed for a more stable peace, we should ascertain that the new strategy *will* provide maximum benefits in a peaceful world. We have managed peace of a sort with previous national strategies; an uneasy peace that, despite all of our investments, has not lessened world tensions. Nor have all these investments even pretended to protect lives during an attack. Assured Survival has the potential to protect most of our civilian population, as we have described. (One U.S. official claims that the Soviets feel a GBMD is worth the investment if it assures the survival of only 40% of its citizens.) The new strategy's potential for peaceful development alone will make it worth its cost.

A global, space-based U.S. defensive umbrella will lessen tensions everywhere, because its peaceful benefits will help solve many of the world's most pressing problems. In this chapter we address some of those benefits. We probably cannot address them all because we are certain to find new advantages as the process unfolds. Council member Robert Heinlein referred to this common phenomenon as the "serendipity benefits" of space development.

Progress is more than possible; it can be a norm. If we are to avoid the gloomy future of so many forecasts, we must find ways to furnish inexpensive energy, materials, and knowledge to have-not nations. Further, we must do it without side effects that pollute our biosphere. We need not, nor can we, do it by apportioning the "pie" of our finite earthly resources into smaller and pathetically smaller slivers so that all suffer equally; we can, however, make a larger pie. And where are we to find a bakery such as will fulfill these desires? Look upward.

The Wealth Of Space Resources

The rest of the Solar System comprises a "pie" so staggeringly vast as to make Earth's resources seem insignificant. We do not have to accept limits to growth when untapped worlds full of resources are near our grasp. The lunar regolith is rich in vital elements, and the Moon has only one-sixth of Earth's gravity. We should have no particular difficulty in setting up extraction equipment on the moon to obtain known raw materials. Indeed, for space activities it will be a better work station than Earth itself. According to Dr. Aldrin, who has experienced all three, that of Earth, space, and the lunar surface, he found the Moon the most congenial of the three locations for working.

Samples of lunar material brought back by Armstrong and Aldrin in 1969, and by our five subsequent lunar landings, provide a fair indication of resources we can expect on the Moon. A partial listing includes:

Oxygen	up to 45%
Silicon	18.7 to 22.4%
Iron	3.5 to 16.9%
Aluminum	4.5 to 14.5%
Calcium	7.7 to 11.2%
Titanium	0.35 to 7.3%
Magnesium	3.9 to 6.3%
Manganese	0.05 to 0.22%
Chromium	0.09 to 0.33%
Sodium	0.23 to 0.52%
Potassium	0.05 to 0.46%
Phosphorus	0.03 to 0.23%

Some of these materials might even prove economically exportable to Earth! The abundant oxygen and the structural metals (iron, aluminum, titanium and magnesium) certainly offer tremendous advantages for lunar development as well as supplies for other missions. A lunar facility can export unprocessed materials cheaply to other locations, and can also export refined material including fully-tested structural hardware just as cheaply.

In terms of its capacity during the next decade or so, the moon is unique and has no competitor. A commercial enterprise that needs low yet significant gravity, hard vacuum, effectively limitless shielding, construction metals and lots of room, will find the Moon unmatched as a commercial base. Unless some new and even more attractive alternative is devised within the next few years—and asteroid capture seems the only significant competing scheme—we will probably see American civilian settlements on the moon. The Soviets have already revealed plans for lunar settlements. We spend perhaps three-tenths of one percent of our gross national product on space, while the Soviets spend about two per cent of theirs on it. If their GNP is only half of ours, they still invest several times as much in space as we do. Their aims are not only military, but economic as well. There is enough wealth in space for all nations; but only if we are allowed free access to it.

The Soviet lunar investment is not well-known in every quarter. Most of the features on the far side of the Moon have Russian names, because Soviet probes mapped those regions before we did. While the Soviets have never placed a human on the lunar surface, their unmanned Lunakhod craft have landed there and carried out science missions, including the return of lunar samples to Soviet scientists on Earth. The Soviets understand as well as we do that lunar bases can cheaply supply plenty of mass for shielding and other purposes, to very large constructs in Earth orbits—including the Lagrange orbits favored by Dr. Gerard O'Neill and others. In exploring more distant celestial bodies, too, manned missions will probably begin from lunar orbit if lunar supply bases are available. Construction, checkout, repair, and much of the supply function can be obtained from local lunar sources, including the lifting of heavy cargo (for example, oxygen and structural parts), much more cheaply than from the Earth. The Moon is clearly destined for settlement in the near future.

Furthermore, in its role as a vast scientific platform, the Moon will provide untold intellectual wealth. Its resources, position, and life-support requirements lend it unique status as a "university" for obtaining the empirical knowledge we need for further expansion into the Solar System. Hemisphere-wide observations of the Earth in "real-time", in combination with the local observations from other satellites, can put earthly meteorology on a new basis.

While no single country can legally claim the moon for its exclusive use, we will soon need to establish its status somewhat more clearly; within a decade or so, nations will be establishing permanent settlements there. (But to do this, they should begin very soon to send more exploratory probes so that those settlements will be at the optimum sites.) International discussions on this topic could cause national leaders to discover the stupendous advantages of collaboration in peaceful space development.

A few careful analysts, meanwhile, do not conclude that the moon is necessarily our one best source of materials. Dr. Eric Drexler has an eye on the increasing number of near-Earth asteroids found by Cal Tech's Helin, Shoemaker, *et al.* Because some of these small planetoids may prove simple to intercept and cheap to take in tow, Drexler cautions that by focusing only on the Moon we could overlook some very attractive sources of raw materials. We simply do not know how many asteroids pass quite near the Earth every year; perhaps up to a thousand. A typical small asteroid of twenty-meter diameter might yield forty million pounds of mass. A single nickel-iron asteroid of one cubic mile—and some of them may exist in near-Earth orbits—could yield more of these metals than Earth produces in a year.

One class of asteroids also contains the carbon and hydrogen lacking in lunar samples, which makes the Helin-Shoemaker studies very much more intriguing; a hydrocarbon-rich asteroid pushed into orbit around the moon would provide elements for lunar development which otherwise would be shipped at great cost from Earth. The same argument holds for seeking water in space. We find growing evidence that many near-Earth asteroids are actually comets, balls of "dirty ice" which may be 60% water. The reduction in cost per ton of water delivered to low-Earth orbit (LEO) could save us billions.

Eventually, when commerce expands to (and beyond) the Asteroid Belt, we will probably be able to mine other planets and satellites for their atmospheric gases, for use in space manufacturing. Given these almost inexhaustible raw materials, we can move from exploration to settlements to cities beyond the Earth; cities that can refine materials and produce consumer goods without any of the attendant pollution that plagues industry and whole populations on Earth today. Best of all, we will not need to wait several generations to begin enjoying some of the fruits of space exploration.

The Birth Of Space Industry

As we might expect, private companies are studying space-derived benefits for profits in the near term. McDonnell-Douglas focuses on electrophoresis for the space manufacture of pharmaceuticals; Westech Systems wants to grow large silicon crystals; Boeing wants a biochemical lab, Battelle Columbus Labs would produce biomedical materials, and GE is looking at the manufacture of latex spheres for blood-flow experiments. Health from space is outlined in more detail in a paper contributed by Drs. Possony and Pournelle (see Appendix).

In addition, Grumman is interested in exotic space-produced crystals for advanced electronics, and Krupp would study magnetic alloys and crystals. A few, including Fairchild and Messerschmitt-Boelkow-Blohm, are already engaged in building platforms for space research and manufacturing. Some large multifunction platforms will be assembled by robots and teleoperation, but serviced as necessary by humans. Other companies likely to obtain early profits from their space investments include Federal Express, Space Services, Orbital Systems Corp., William Sword, Inc., Tran-Space Carriers, Eagle Engineering, Pacific American Launch Systems, Star-struck, Inc., and Stiennon and Partners. Hughes and RCA, of course, already make satellites for many purposes.

Perhaps the most popular example of a peaceful return on our Assured Survival investment is that of the Solar Power Satellite (SPS). We have been powering satellites with solar cells for many years, and we would need no scientific breakthroughs to build robot-assembled, miles-wide solar panels in space. In fact, our atmosphere impedes sunlight so much that a solar cell can produce about eight times as much electricity in Earth orbit as it does at sea level.

Our sixteen-kilowatt solar cell system for Skylab was the largest power source ever put in orbit by anyone. A twenty-five kilowatt unit in orbit could augment shuttle power and, of course, something of the sort will be needed early in the construction of space stations. Following these pilot-plant demonstration units, an SPS would be no more than a very large engineering project, perhaps on the order of a major suspension bridge, and could narrowly beam its power down to microwave receiving antennae on Earth. The price of that continuous electrical power would be competitive with present generating plants that worry us so much with their pollution. And it would be just as cheap to bring that power directly to, say, Africa or India, as to beam it to the U.S. India alone could use scores of these orbiting power plants, and with power this cheap, even India could afford it.

We are often told how energy shortages prompt third-world farmers to use all their biomass as fuel, which eventually turns their arable land into wasteland. We are also told by some that through intelligent self-interest if not altruism, we must help the tens of millions of people who face famine because they have denuded their countrysides for energy. The SPS might be, not only the best, but the cheapest, and in the long run perhaps the only answer. It would permit us to offer options of clean, inexpensive power to other countries for their use, as they need it. In effect, we would make it possible for them to create wealth of their own without heavy-handed interference. This is exactly the kind of commercial enterprise that can grow within a generation from permanent outposts in Earth orbit.

Lunar and more ambitious missions launched from the proximity of a manned orbiting station will benefit from the same rationale that currently explains the launch of commercial satellites from our shuttle. The mission craft can be assembled, checked out, and launched from space under the watchful eyes of nearby project scientists.

Some Council members debate the absolute requirement for orbital space stations, citing teleoperation and robotics systems that could replace humans in the operational loop. Others reply that missile silos, early-warning radars, and lighthouses still need humans close by and, at least for the near future, we will need humans at the site of our large space assets. The question of absolute requirement, by now, is moot; we can expect to see one or more space stations before we see some of the other essentials of a GBMD program.

Given this likelihood, we suggest that external tanks for the present shuttles be jettisoned in orbit, rather than letting them fall into the Indian Ocean. *It will take less fuel to carry these huge external tanks (79,000 pounds each) to orbit than it now takes to cast them into the sea.* With low-mass tethers, and without any further nudging to higher orbit, the tanks can remain in orbit for 20 or 30 years. With some modification, several of them could become the framework for a space station, complete with the imparted spin to provide "artificial gravity" for long-term occupancy. Several other uses for orbiting shuttle tanks come to mind for peaceful uses, including emergency habitats and storage of industrial materials. Waste not, want not!

Manned Presence And Telepresence

Another rationale for continuous manned presence in our space assets is that sabotage of a manned vehicle is a much more serious violation of the peace than damage to an unmanned system—the difference between vandalism and piracy. Yet we should explicitly state that it will be easier for us to pursue some missions by teleoperation.

Teleoperation is an array of techniques for using the senses of a human operator with sophisticated sensors and communication links to perform remote operations. Among the best-known of early teleoperator devices are the remote metal "hands" used to handle radioactive materials (called "Waldoes", after a story by Robert Heinlein). Many simple tasks such as guiding an unmanned vehicle slowly across the lunar surface, or straightforward lunar mining operations, might be performed today with tele-operation. It would involve less risk to humans, and less expense, because the human operator could be sitting in an office on Earth. Yet we would not be restrained by the intelligence which we can build into a robot because, already, teleoperator systems can combine computers and humans. The remote manipulator arm of our shuttle (RMS) is an operational teleoperator system.

The remote human operator needs a sense of presence at the site of the operation, dubbed "telepresence". With correct force feedback and video transmission, the operator can perform many tasks as well as if he were present at the remote site. Much of the original research into teleoperation was completed in 1965, and in 1983 the Council's Dr. Marvin Minsky participated in MIT's update of the state of the art. The reports (to NASA) are under the code name ARAMIS. At the present state of the art, teleoperators need better picture transmission for many tasks. With the proper mix of humans and teleoperation, however, the U.S. could use off-the-shelf techniques to complete virtually all of the construction for proposed Earth-orbital engineering projects.

Teleoperation techniques will play a large part in peaceful space development, yet their relatively advanced state is not very widely known. Ken Salisbury of Stanford has developed a controller with seven degrees of freedom, used at JPL (Jet Propulsion Labs). Fine teleoperator arms are now marketed by Carl Flatteau, and similar arms are available at JPL for experiments. Bell Helicopter's Hugh Upton was first to develop a Head-Aimed Television (HAT) display. Both John Chatten and Honeywell have developed HATs, while the Navy is said to have both a HAT and master/slave arms attached to a submersible vehicle. International Submarine Engineering of Vancouver also has master/slave arms and controllers for sale. General Electric's E. L. Mosher developed man-amplifier machines and teleoperators, dubbed "Hardi-man" and "Handi-man."

Force-amplifiers are particularly interesting, since the machines can employ very much more strength than a man's muscles in performing hard labor. Pound-for-pound, though, muscles are still more efficient than motors. The jumping leg of a grasshopper, for example, can apply two kilograms of force against the ground, and can do it repeatedly. Eric Kolm of Piezoelectric Products is developing piezoelectric muscle said to have five times the energy density of electric motors, with direct conversion of electric energy to linear motion. Contractile plastics may yet replace electric motors in teleoperator devices.

In brief, then, teleoperation and robotics are sufficiently advanced to be immediately useful in space. Council members William Haynes and James Ransom have already made time-and-motion studies of space-suited humans compared to these alternative systems. Highly repetitive tasks such as assembly of SPS panels might best be relegated to automated devices, while troubleshooting of a satellite would probably require human presence.

Another inevitable spinoff of GBMD will be civilian applications of military supercomputers and their programs. These will range from medical diagnosis to mining to air and ground traffic control systems. With a sufficiently advanced artificial intelligence, we can probably supplant many teleoperator devices with completely independent robots.

Commercial Space Vehicles

Our extraterrestrial construction projects will need vehicles that lift their payloads more cheaply than current systems. It is the Council's unanimous opinion that it will be cheaper for the government to request bids for transportation of supplies to space assets, rather than continuing with new government-developed heavy-lift launch vehicles indefinitely. After all, the government already accepts bids for commercial transportation of military supplies to

Europe. Furthermore, and this is very important, a guaranteed market for space transport might do for the future of space commerce what guaranteed air-mail contracts did for early commercial airlines. We already have more missions requested through 1986 than we can meet with our tiny fleet of shuttles. The European Ariane IV craft may become the only re-course for some users if we cannot serve their needs. This is not to malign the excellence of the shuttles; we need more of them! But we will need other vehi-cles soon, and development should commence, at least at the proposal level now.

Private industry representatives, including mem-bers of this council, claim that single-stage-to-orbit (SSTO) cargo vehicles capable of four trips per day are perfectly feasible with current technology. Some designers estimate that an SSTO of modest size and five-ton payload could be developed for under $500 million and a small fleet of them could lift payloads to orbit for a startlingly low price: $5 per pound. The current price: nearer $5,000 dollars per pound. This fleet could place a million *tons* in orbit in four years for a total cost of about $1.5 billion. And once into orbit, a payload can be moved to many other places, such as the moon, relatively cheaply.

But SSTOs are only the beginning of the future of flight. Extremely high-powered lasers, following their development as GBMD weapons, can probably be used to propel cargo vehicles to orbit as we men-tioned in Chapter 2. The laser propulsion system has two potentially decisive advantages for commercial space developments. First, because the energy source can be remote, the vehicle can carry more payload and less fuel. Second, the energy source can be electrical, bringing the cost-per-pound-to-orbit down to levels competitive with airlines. Braced with the cost figures on projected laser propulsion systems, some analysts say—only half-joking—that orbital ho-tels for tourists may have to lease their own SSTO shuttles as courtesy buses to handle the traffic.

Several other nations (France, Japan, etc.) have

proven their ability to loft orbital payloads for commercial uses; if the policies of the U.S. Government become highly restrictive other nations will cheerfully undersell us. In the past, sales of commercial U.S. aircraft have been a major contributor to a favorable balance of trade. Commercial U.S. spacecraft sales can do the same in the future. Some industry spokesmen say that our government need not use special incentives to motivate U.S. firms to compete in space businesses; it will be enough if the government simply refrains from placing *dis*incentives in their way.

We expect other peaceful spinoffs from laser weapon technology, particularly the free electron laser. With efficiencies that may approach 50%, and extremely high average power operation, FELs are not limited to a given wavelength and have many potential applications both on Earth and in space. They could be used to transmit power across very great distances with little loss, and have great potential in industrial processing such as isotope separation.

Small Businesses And Small Problems

Perhaps now is the time to begin thinking of ways to include that driving force of the American economy, the small entrepreneur. The peaceful civilian applications of space development will quickly involve niches for some relatively small businesses, and we may expect complaints that large consortiums are usurping those "small slots". A commercial firm could supply a map of any spot, at any scale, by photography and/or computer enhancement, even to show a farmer where his irrigation is less than perfect, or where disease is affecting his crops. A service group could pinpoint a lost child or even a pet if it were instrumented—or if IR sensors are sufficiently improved through GBMD development.

As peaceful commercial opportunities become broader in space, we will probably have to review treaties for interpretation and, if necessary, revision.

The Outer Space Treaty of 1967 requires continuing supervision by governments of private enterprise, but the scope of this supervision must be made clearer as commercial opportunities grow. Question: What should private enterprise *not* be allowed to do in space?

The liability for damages caused by a commercial space object should also be addressed. The likelihood of such damage is quite small but it remains a possibility. The simplest way to satisfy international liability agreements may be to obtain an agreement between the U.S. Government and the operators of private U.S. space firms. The firm would agree to insure its operations for third-party liability to some amount agreed upon by the government and the firm.

The peaceful benefits of our exploration of space and development of space assets range from mapping services, through sale and lease of commercial spacecraft, to new revenues for insurance companies. And as Mr. Heinlein observed, we have yet to discover more than a small fraction of the serendipity benefits.

The Ultimate Benefit

Perhaps the most underestimated and least-discussed benefit of our peaceful expansion into space will be the motivation of our people. A vigorous new program designed to maximize peaceful benefits will recapture the imagination of the American public. It will have a huge impact on our scientific and technical education systems, drawing the best and brightest of our youth into science-oriented careers. The result could be an American Renaissance.

CHAPTER SEVEN

Streamlining The Teams

Though much work remains to be done, we have shown that our technology is capable of providing the hardware for Mutual Assured Survival. In recent years, however, we have suffered restrictions in the ponderous plumbing of bureaucracy. Even though consensus is growing as to the new strategic defense, the best avenues of approach are not clear in detail. If we are to pursue our new national strategy in economical fashion, we must streamline the ways in which we manage our space programs.

The Pentagon's process for acquiring new hardware, for example, has become notoriously bloated. Good programs can be studied to death, perfected to death, and/or managed to death, by overlapping agencies whose personnel are overly interested in expanding and protecting their bureaucratic "turf."

But we know that we can overcome these problems; we have overcome them before. The U.S. Army Engineers ran their Manhattan District efficiently during the development of the atomic bomb, which took under three years. More recently the USAF's

139

Western Development Division, under General Bernard Schriever, developed our initial ballistic missiles in very brief spans. Our first Polaris SLBMs went from drawing board to ocean deployment in four years despite technical problems that were not known to be solvable when we started. Our most stunning achievement, the Apollo lunar landings, were achieved in roughly eight years, in part because most of NASA was pre-empted for that goal. The Apollo program managers had exceptional powers which allowed them to circumvent many bureaucratic obstacles.

A generation ago, we managed these startling space achievements because our programs were run by hard-charging pioneer organizations like the USAF Space Division and NASA. Now, both are slow-moving bureaucracies. It seems unlikely that any of our existing directorates will set its affairs in order enough to manage big new space programs with economy and dispatch. For one thing, an agency which manages other and older programs as well, may tend to have priorities it favors over a genuinely *de*fensive GBMD. For another, government agencies often spend more time studying a new program than they spend to develop it. Generally speaking, the U.S. Government today takes three times as long as it takes the commercial sector to make a new system operational. Older agencies tend to overstaff for a given task, even after a system becomes operational. Does NASA really need a thousand people to supervise a dozen shuttle launches a year?

The basic problem in most government R & D programs is an elaborate system of study, definition, competition, and recompetition. This procedure may be appropriate for new systems of low urgency, where cost-effectiveness may not be paramount, as compared, say, to maintaining high levels of employment, but for anything approaching the urgency of a global defensive umbrella, this is a stupid approach. What we need is something more like the Manhattan Project. Organize swiftly; give contracts to essential contributors; isolate the talent in secure locations; at crucial decision nodes take both paths; work around the clock. For somewhat less urgency, the Apollo model may be best. Set the goals; complete procurement paperwork; choose contractors; develop preliminary designs; then follow with system development, tests, and operations. If studies are necessary to pinpoint optimum approaches or engineering details, they can be made a part of the systems engineering process.

Compare current NASA practice. First, the agency conducts feasibility studies. The results are then endlessly reviewed by various committees. Eventually contractors are selected to conduct competitive preliminary design studies. With these designs in hand (four or five years after starting the feasibility studies), the agency organizes procurement of development-type hardware. During this development phase, the agency's review committees keep the contractors off-balance as to whether the government is still really serious about the program (this, naturally, tends to make any wary contractor want to minimize his commitment). Often, the agency also hires "think-tank" contractors who urge the agency to change the program's objectives and even its design requirements during the development program. The result: several years' delay, and horrendous cost overruns. If we are several years late with GBMD, we will be too late, period.

We need a new agency, formed from scratch. Why? First, most volunteers step forward because they enjoy change, challenge, and innovation; they have good tolerance for uncertainty. They tend to have adequate self-assurance and are stimulated by the job.

Second, management guidelines are broad; they have not had a chance to be cast in bronze. Innovative management is virtually unavoidable; the details of management are conducted more to meet the task than to upholster a career.

Third, the top echelons have not had decades to develop the kind of monitoring procedures that can and usually do insulate them from the program. Supervision often deals directly with the top echelons, and communication on all levels is improved.

Fourth, management generally has not developed *a priori* positions, has few mistakes to hide, and only embryonic vested interests to protect. Success is measured by the meeting of program goals, often in innovative ways, without undue regard for the status quo.

Compare the above to the typical operation of a middle-aged agency like NASA. The evolution of shuttle space suit, or EMU (extravehicular mobility unit), is a case in point.

In 1976, NASA originally budgeted $17.9 million for roughly twenty suits, five backpack life support systems, test equipment, and trained specialists to maintain the hardware. The EMU was intended as a significant advance beyond Apollo and Skylab suits, with superior mobility and easy resizing for astronauts. The million-dollar suit, sized for one astronaut, was to be a thing of the past. Or was it?

At the end of Fiscal Year 1983, runout costs of the EMU program were just under *$300 million*. The few flight-ready units need 170 people to maintain them, and fitting the standard parts to an astronaut takes several man-days of tailoring—in part because the components were designed to fit a very great range of astronaut body sizes, from a 5th percentile female to a 95th percentile male. And despite this richly-funded project, the hardware is inferior to a suit developed in a parallel NASA program in which two men spent a total of $150,000 a year.

The superior suit is the AX-3, which has better mobility and can be resized in minutes. An astronaut can get into or out of it in five minutes without help; it is cheaper to manufacture and maintain; and because of its constant-volume design, the suit is pressurized to 8 psi without severely restricting the astronaut's movements. This relatively high pressure allows an astronaut to go from sea-level cabin pressure to vacuum without suffering from the "bends". In repeated tests in 1982, NASA found that its $300 million suits posed a hazard to some wearers because of the low suit pressure (under 5 psi) when exiting from sea-level cabin pressure. At this writing it still remains to be seen whether NASA will soon switch to some version of the safer, cheaper, high-pressure AX-3 suit. In all fairness we repeat that the AX-3 suit is also a NASA development, but in view of NASA's apparent determination to use the expensive suit, one cynic asked in mock innocence whether NASA was in business to protect astronauts or investments!

The AX-3 is only one of numerous programs which yielded strikingly superior results from streamlined teams. In France, Dassault assembles only 200 top people to develop highly successful fighter aircraft. From sheet metal specialists to preliminary designers, all are the best available. The result is a flyable prototype.

In the U.S., Lockheed's Kelly Johnson used a similar approach in the "Skunk Works" to produce the U-2 and SR-71 aircraft. Dr. Paul MacCready, with resources so small as to defy belief, developed true breakthrough aircraft in his Gossamer series of man-powered aircraft and his sun-powered Solar Challenger.

Burt Rutan and Ames Research Corporation have built and flown a series of light research aircraft for less money than large aerospace corporations had asked to do preliminary design studies. The Ames team is small, highly skilled, and like the MacCready team, highly motivated.

All of these efforts point to leaner, highly motivated groups that develop superior systems without wasting time or money. They do *not* imply that every new development should proceed without studying previous work. In the case of a GBMD program, we may already have useful designs that were shelved and then forgotten.

During the past decade or so, the U.S. has shelved programs after considerable research and, in some cases, the development of experimental hardware.

We should determine whether the data was destroyed and, if it is available, review it. We could quickly determine which useful ideas we can resurrect, and which avenues we need not duplicate. It is entirely reasonable to suspect that some important prior work on missile defense has been suppressed or destroyed. In the past, in line with MacNamara's dictum that we must not have ABMs, some of our scientific community advised that *all research on defenses against ICBMs must be suppressed*. Though this advice was not always followed, it may have caused the suppression of concepts, analyses, even experimental hardware, *particularly if it seemed promising*. It seems very unlikely that we will unearth any fully developed weapons; those charged with suppression of research would almost certainly have branded the ideas as "impossible" or "not cost-effective" long before the demonstration stage.

We might, for example, examine early nuclear propulsion systems such as Project ORION and Dumbo with a view toward very fast deployment of massive systems in orbit. At this point, we simply cannot guess what crucial data might be slumbering in the technological cemetaries of NASA and DoD. It may, however, prove a rich source of innovative GBMD schemes.

We place heavy emphasis on innovation because our R & D establishment generally does *not*, and we will need innovative techniques to erect a GBMD without undue delay. Nowhere is this more true than in the field of weapons development. Weapon program leaders are usually satisfied with conservative, steady improvement. For the most part, imaginative departures are not wanted, so they are not obtained. In many cases it is true that an imaginative new idea will not make a given system meet its design goals significantly better; but that idea might have been of great significance in another program. We need some forum for GBMD innovation.

A forum directed toward rewarding innovative GBMD ideas should probably be separate from the main R & D organization. We gain the potential for "leapfrogging" expensive steps in research or development. This happens seldom; but when it happens, the savings in time and money can be enormous.

This kind of forum has been available in the past. The Defense Advanced Research Projects Agency (DARPA) was a major source of DoD innovation, and NASA innovations often emerged from Office of Applications and Space Technology (OAST) centers. Indeed, a few requests still emerge from NASA (e.g., recently from Marshall Center) soliciting highly innovative schemes from individual scientists known to be on the forefront of technology. But generally the OAST centers have now inherited conservative programs, restricting their ability to study innovative technology.

We might regain some innovative thrust by expanding DARPA into a broader ARPA, though innovation often works best in organizations smaller than that. We might also designate one of the NASA centers toward this focus; it is important to recognize that NASA and DoD often compete, though they share the need for innovation in several core technologies.

The military, commerce, and science are linked by their mutual need for several common core technologies. The government must provide access to space, and reasonable security for investments there. It is vital that we have maximum sharing of innovative schemes in such areas as zero-gravity processing; surveying and processing of extraterrestrial materials; producing and storing propellants; and safety of human-rated systems, including solar shielding.

Certainly, some details of GBMD strategy will interact with regard to hardware and core technologies. Technical problems common to several details can be studied in parallel so that the program can "run lean, run fast" for less expenditures of time and money. Our present structures of organization and management are not streamlined. The new ones must:

• use goal-oriented management with rigorously enforced deadlines;

• organize project teams in a matrix that links them by technology, function, strategy, and responsibility;

• streamline security procedures to aggressively promote communication among the teams for information sharing; and

• recruit the best people available and provide them with the resources to do their jobs.

Our view of existing bureaucracies, then, is not a very flattering one. We doubt that old organizations can erect a GBMD with the verve we desperately need. Still, NASA might be revitalized. It could share control with its customers; USAF, USN, National Science Foundation, and so on. Some of this control could come from an external council for oversight planning. NASA could standardize much hardware and eliminate duplication of effort by all users, military and commercial. It could, from the top downward, work to minimize its internal rivalries. It could avoid huge cost overruns that often emerge from sole-source supplier monopolies. It could take more active measures toward innovation. It could turn some of its operational work over to private industry, providing U.S. commerce with a nucleus of people who can support our future commerce in space. NASA could, with proper direction, become lean and vigorous.

Whatever agencies we employ for our revitalized space programs, we must have a U.S. space development strategy that coordinates both military and civilian space efforts including programs on the Moon and beyond. Military planners can then build on existing programs and, in turn, contribute to commercial developments. This is the strategy that made the U.S. a world leader in military aircraft and air commerce. If we intend to be leaders in space, we must begin by streamlining our management teams.

CHAPTER EIGHT

Snipers

Our advances in space have proven popular with Americans and their Allies—especially after the fact. The military programs which led to our peaceful spacefaring, and without which we would now be a third-rate power, have not enjoyed as much popularity. Assured Survival has already drawn fire from several quarters, much of it centered on the idea of placing weapons in space. We should study this sniping, if only to understand the motivations behind it.

While some military experts are enthusiastic about a space-based defense, the Pentagon houses some opposition, notably among program managers of offensive weapon systems. General Graham, long familiar with the Pentagon bureaucracy, points out that a public forum was necessary if his High Frontier GBMD was to survive this opposition. Some Pentagon program managers remain hostile to the new strategy because it promises to divert funds, and importance, from their programs. When we ask these managers for an objective view of a strategy which protects

147

civilians while limiting offensive weapon programs, we probably ask too much. Even when Pentagon planners converge on the new strategy, we will probably see some efforts to keep near-term solutions from appearing too attractive (a benign description of this ploy might be "professional courtesy"). Assured Survival will probably draw less sniper fire from the Pentagon as more truly *de*fensive programs get underway there. This is not to say that rivalries will cease, but that opposition to bold new ideas tends to subside as the new programs gain momentum.

McGeorge Bundy, a national security official during the Kennedy and Johnson administrations, argued in 1983 against the new strategy on technical grounds. In the pages of the *Washington Post,* Bundy debated with Dr. Arnold Kramish (Council member and a Fellow at the Smithsonian's Woodrow Wilson Center). Bundy agreed that we must continue to search for ways to change ". . . the terrible reality . . ." of MAD, adding, ". . . I specifically endorsed research on military defense." Yet Mr. Bundy denied that the U.S. had any scientific basis for hope that we are ready to develop a GBMD. Of President Reagan's call for an effective missile defense, Bundy said, "Was there any serious consultation at all with experts and leaders in the scientific community? Apparently not." In fairness to Mr. Bundy we recognize that he meant *prior* consultation.

But Kramish replied, in part, "I do challenge that President Reagan's action was not based on . . . careful assessment of technological development . . ." and suggested that Reagan's understanding of the technology was equivalent to Roosevelt's understanding of fission. The focus of this debate may be secondary to a related question: regardless of prior consultations, *are* we technologically ready to develop a GBMD?

Senator Sam Nunn (D-Georgia), in July of 1983, remarked that he could find no expert who feels that the American people could be protected by missile defenses. He has since learned that there are many such experts. Unfortunately, the opponents of BMD, and those who speak of "STAR WARS," get most of the press.

Dr. Kosta Tsipis of MIT, writing in various media, has attacked missile defense ideas on grounds of our technical limitations. From several quarters, other physicists promptly reported that Tsipis's analyses are so riddled with flaws as to sink beneath serious notice. For example, Tsipis argued that a beam weapon is limited by plasma interference in air; but laser physicists say that the numbers Tsipis quoted were inexcusably wrong, literally by several orders of magnitude. Widely published frequent errors are a way to court professional suicide. We avidly welcome further publications by Dr. Tsipis.

This book is an attempted demonstration of our technological readiness to begin developing a missile defense. Now let us cite experts who are recognized at the Congressional testimony level—even if some critics cannot "find" them.

Dr. John D. G. Rather, of D. S. E. Research and Engineering, was previously a physicist at Oak Ridge and Lawrence Livermore as well as a radio astronomer at the National Radio Astronomy Observatory. Rather believes that the free electron laser could lead directly to laser weapon systems and to major civilian space applications as well. He estimates that, if we pursue several programs at once, we could have a *deployed* U.S. laser weapon system by 1990. Incidentally, he suggests that in developing space-based defenses, we do as the Soviets do: maintain a massive R & D effort with no announced purpose beyond civilian developments. In this way, both the U.S. and the Soviets can erect nearly all components of their missile defenses without overt threatening gestures. Rather's implication is unmistakeable; if the Soviets are not already grooming their BMD, they have mislaid the ace up their sleeve.

Dr. Lowell Wood, a physicist at Lawrence Livermore on Dr. Edward Teller's staff, has said that an ABM system would take us about a decade; *not* because of the technical challenge, but only because the U.S. is not yet serious about the effort. A serious effort, which would shorten the delay by years, was outlined in Chapter 6.

Dr. Maxwell Hunter of Lockheed (and the "gang of four"), stated flatly in 1977 that beam weapons were already proliferating and were so potentially decisive in missile defense that this defense should be pursued with all due haste.

Dr. George Keyworth, physicist and science advisor to President Reagan, reports that after a year's study of the technology, the White House Science Panel found no major fundamental barriers to a layered missile defense system.

The Soviets, of course, do not challenge a GBMD on technological grounds. Yuri Andropov, with developed killer satellites and BMD radars near completion (in addition to upgarded nuclear-tipped ABMs deployed around Moscow), took the opposite tack. He charged that a U.S. defensive umbrella is a bid to disarm the Soviet Union. The heat of a Soviet denunciation, combined with their own advanced systems, suggests that they, perhaps better than anyone else, know how close both sides are to developing a GBMD capability.

In reply to Andropov's charge, we can only repeat what we have already said: no system is perfect. Our GBMD would not "disarm" the Soviets if it intercepted half, or even nine-tenths, of their nuclear warheads. Nor would Soviet missile defenses disarm us. We only wish this kind of total disarmament *were* feasible—but we know better, and so did Mr. Andropov. The best any nation can do is to provide Assured Survival for most of its civilian population. We cannot fault Mr. Andropov for having done so, and we propose to do the same.

Another group of critics of Assured Survival, in the West as well as the Soviet Bloc, follow a line similar to Andropov's; i.e., that an American GBMD would be destabilizing. A domestic broadcast from Moscow on 19 August 1983 announced to Soviet listeners that: "After all, it was none other than President

Reagan who made a speech in March this year, which shocked all sensible people since it dealt with something unthinkable, which used to be the prerogative of fantasy-mongers—namely, war in space."

Of course, with virtually total control of their media, Soviet leaders can prevent their citizens from knowing the details of their own space weapons—the world's *only* operational satellite-killers. If we took the Soviet broadcaster at his word, we could only conclude either that Soviet leaders had already shocked themselves, or that they are not "sensible people." We prefer to consider them unshocked and sensible.

In the Soviet periodical *Aviation & Cosmonautics*, June 1983, Colonel V. Bykovskiy voiced a common objection to space weapons. Bykovskiy, a pilot-cosmonaut, warned of hostilities in space: "And truly war in space is much more dangerous than on Earth, since its consequences can lead via unavoidable processes to the end of life on our planet."

But if it ever came to that, every weapon targeted against another in space would be a weapon that would NOT kill masses of civilians on Earth. It is the premise of Assured Survival that most weapons passing through space on their way to Earth will be nullified there. The end of life on Earth is readily avoidable; even in the event of war, we propose, in the words of one council member, to kill missiles, not people.

It is often difficult to focus on Soviet arguments without amusement at their bogus innocence. On 21 August 1983, a domestic Moscow broadcast panel warned of a space arms race. Dmitri A. Volskiy remarked, on the subject of arms limitations: "Yes, our position is precise, clear, frank, honest, consistent, and principled. The Soviet Union does not intend to intimidate anyone."

Perhaps comrade Volskiy meant, as with the SS-20s they brandish against frightened Europeans, they do not intend to intimidate anyone until it is too late for the other side to do anything about it.

On the same panel, Vadim N. Nekrasov ended with this charge: "Washington wants to play without any rules in the hope that it will thereby achieve military superiority and dictate its terms to the Soviet Union. This is undoubtedly another miscalculation, a miscalculation that is dangerous not only for America but also for the whole world, since, if the plans for putting modern weapons into space were implemented, the arms race would take on such a monstrous shape that it is even difficult to talk about it at present."

But when the U.S. did have clear superiority, we did not dictate terms. Instead, for nearly a decade, we stopped the increase of our major offensive systems, ICBMs and bombers, while the Soviets overtook us. Also, Nekrasov is either ignorant of operational Soviet space weapons, or he considers their one-sided advantage non-monstrous. In any event we fully agree that for Comrade Nekrasov or any other Soviet analyst, their own space weapons are "difficult to talk about" on Radio Moscow.

Even if forced to acknowledge their weapons, they can easily define any new Soviet weapon as "stabilizing," and any counter as "destabilizng". Media theorists recognize that such arguments are highly persuasive to an audience that is kept naive as a matter of rigid policy. It is more difficult to understand how, with access to information on all sides, any serious Western analyst would conclude that American defenses against missiles are warlike, while Soviet weapons are all peaceable. It is much easier to believe that persuasion, not realistic analysis, is their goal.

It is fairly obvious, given the consistent Soviet styles of antiweapon rhetoric and steady weapon development, that we need other than verbal assurances. We must pursue a course that is in the best interest of civilian populations. If possible, we must also negotiate with the Soviets so that both sides can lower the end costs of weaponry; can prevent horrendous accidents on any side; and can objectively verify what an opponent swears to. No one can verify compliance of a treaty, for example, when it permits on-site inspection only after advance warning. Anyone who has ever seen military service knows the difference: with advance warning of inspection, you clean up to hide your dirty work. With unannounced inspection, you don't do much dirty work.

A few critics of GBMD admit its advantages but shrink from its costs. We find the costs minuscule, when we consider either war or peace. In a war—perhaps *especially* an accidental one—every city saved from obliteration is a mass of people worth the entire effort. And what is it worth to significantly reduce the chances of nuclear war altogether? Without war, the scientific and commercial benefits springing from space development can revitalize the world's economies and give hope to nations which never had economies, nor indeed much hope. Still, in previous chapters we acknowledge that costs *are* a proper subject for serious criticism. At each meeting of the Citizens Advisory Council on National Space Policy, a committee convenes to suggest more economical ways to achieve space goals.

Some members of our scientific community, notably Carl Sagan and others in the National Research Council (NRC), have always opposed any space development that involved manned missions. They will oppose a GBMD; they will probably oppose manned space stations, even without a military connection, just as readily as they opposed the Mercury and Apollo missions. They will probably oppose lunar settlements, even though scientific research has profited enormously from our earlier manned space missions. Their opposition stems chiefly from the fear that the expense of man-rated systems will restrict funding for 'pure' space research. These critics may, by now, have profited again from "hands-on" repair of the malfunctioning Solar Max satellite by the crew of the shuttle they opposed.

We do not expect any amount of this proof-of-practicality to soon dampen NRC hostility. It is perfectly obvious that manned missions imply the possibility of exploiting the resources of the Solar System by commerce and applied science rather than an exclusive series of probes totally controlled by an exclusive group of scientists. We will need probes and pure science—but in any event the NRC will not maintain the Solar System as a preserve for its private study. Soviet expansion into space, with or without our own, will soon see to that.

We suspect that some scientific opposition to manned missions is purely (!) *pro forma*, an attempt to maintain a balance between manned and unmanned space efforts. Scientists surely cannot long deny the value and the glory of humanity's expansion into space. Otherwise, why would Dr. Carl Sagan so cheerfully pilot his own interstellar craft through billions and billions of stars in the imaginative *Cosmos* broadcasts?

In summary, most of the sniping against GBMD can be put in opposite categories. One extreme view is that we are not technologically ready to begin. The other extreme view is that we are so technologically advanced that we can use a GBMD to bully the rest of the world. We propose that adherents of these opposing views engage in a fruitful dialogue, so that both positions can be rationally modified while we and other nations erect defenses for our vulnerable populations.

CHAPTER NINE

Q.E.D.

"The President's defensive technologies initiative is a spectacularly ambitious one. Quite simply, it will require a scientific, technical, military, and organizational undertaking that will dwarf anything ever before mounted by the human race . . .

"I believe that mutual assured destruction is a morally bankrupt philosophy that places Government in the untenable position of refusing to defend its citizenry. What the President has proposed is no less than a moral recovery in American strategic policy which would take us from the horror of MAD to the promise of mutual assured protection. It is a goal which deserves the fervent support of all who yearn for a world safe from nuclear weapons. Unless we are willing to accept the prospect of a nuclear Pearl Harbor from space, we must now join the President in a new national commitment to mutual assured protection."
—Representative Ken Kramer, R-Colorado, 1983.

No single work can address all the aspects of Assured Survival. As Representative Kramer notes, this is a vast undertaking, one with few parallels in human history.

The most complex task in all human history was Project Apollo. Hundreds of thousands of people, most working independently, had to accomplish their tasks to a rigid schedule that culminated in a roar of fire at the Kennedy Space Center in Florida on a muggy summer morning.

Prior to Apollo, humanity's most complex task was Overlord: the Normandy invasion. Indeed, throughout human history the most complex activities, and the largest undertakings, have been military operations—which is why the nation had to put generals and admirals in charge of Project Apollo. No one else, not even the heads of the largest corporations, had ever managed anything so complex.

If Apollo accomplished nothing else, it set a new record: the most complex action in human history culminated in a plaque proudly proclaiming that "We came in peace for all mankind."

For more than thirty years we have devoted fantastic energies to building weapons of destruction. It is small wonder that we will not easily render those weapons obsolete and irrelevant. That will take much time and work—but it is a work worth doing.

Critics will inevitably proclaim this work to be incomplete. They will be correct. Any single work claiming completely to cover the topic of Assured Survival would be naive, disingenuous, or in a handsome thirty-six volume set, ten years late. None of us can afford any of those options because we are already several years late in discarding an all-offensive strategy. We all need to understand, *now*, that our population has an alternative to being hostage.

The Soviet Union has always deployed the best possible defenses. They are, they say, the very purpose of government. Moreover, every Soviet citizen undergoes compulsory instruction in Civil Defense—

not, the Soviets say, because they believe they can and should fight a nuclear war, but because it would be criminal not to save as many of their citizens as possible in the event that war comes despite their best intentions.

When they consider other nation's defenses they have a different attitude. Their official response to President Reagan's Strategic Defense Initiatives speech was:

"All attempts at gaining military superiority over the U.S.S.R. are futile. The Soviet Union will never allow them to succeed. It will never be caught defenseless by any threat.

"Let there be no mistake about this in Washington. It is time they stopped devising one option after another in search of the best ways of unleashing nuclear war in the hopes of winning it. Engaging in this is not just irresponsible, it is insane." (Yuri Andropov, interview, *Pravda* March 27, 1983)

Simultaneously the Soviets called for a nuclear freeze, to be verified by "existing national means of verification"; ie., by space satellites. There would be no inspections. There never are in Soviet proposals.

The alternatives are clear. We can continue the doctrine of MAD, or we can move off that sterile path.

MAD promises survival through assurance of destruction. At best MAD promises a world much like the past, fraught with nuclear terror. Our alternative, Assured Survival, looks to a better world. It also promises to enrich us all in peacetime; and it can save most of Earth's civilian populations in the event of war. At the risk of too much repetition: Assured Survival does not claim to be an invulnerable umbrella. A global ballistic missile defense could not save 100% of war victims any more than seat belts, dual brake systems, and energy-absorbent chassis can save 100% of accident victims. This uncertainty is one of the chief stabilizing factors of a GBMD; it provides us with relief, but not arrogance.

A GBMD will not be erected as a single event, but as a series of defensive systems, preferably beginning with interim "now-tech" defenses as soon as possible. We must, in the meantime, develop various high-tech solutions such as defensive beam weapons that cannot be misconstrued as offensive weapons of mass destruction. We must be able to protect our assets both in low Earth orbit (LEO) and where many of our commercial assets are already stationed in geo-synchronous orbit (GEO).

Just as our European Allies originally asked for Pershing II and Tomahawk cruise missiles to counter new Soviet weapons, we believe they will welcome a space-based shield—though this welcome may not become general until it is unmistakeably clear that the Soviets have been developing such a shield themselves. Because the U.S. start will be later than that of the Soviets, we should welcome help from our Allies in developing the West's GBMD for the general welfare.

We should make our defensive aims clear to the Soviets through the treaty process, while maintaining a clear understanding of one advantage their closed society confers: secrecy. Their press and their travel are restricted far more than ours. We must work with the Soviets to achieve real verifications of every paragraph of every agreement. If we cannot do this, every treaty is another Soviet advantage. If we adhere to an unverifiable agreement, we probably lose because if they can they surely will violate it in secrecy. If we attempt similar violations, we almost surely lose because our free press and our freedom of travel means discovery of our violation. Without powerful means for verification, to the Soviets a treaty is like a piñata, made so they can break it and get all the goodies.

Another repetition: we do not fault the Soviets for military aspects of their initial spacefaring. We only fault them for duplicity in their double standard. The future of the human race depends on human assets beyond our biosphere, and any nation with competitors must see to the security of those assets. We intend to see to the security of ours. We might wish for a better scenario, but we will not achieve it. Lacking synergism with initial military developments in space, the United States could not later become economically competitive there.

It is vital that we, as a nation, show enthusiasm for space development; our economic growth depends as much on this optimism as on our great capability. We are already seeing economic competition for shuttle space that taxes our present operations. There is more demand for launches than we can supply, and several nations are vying for this growing market. Japan is investigating the possibility of buying an American shuttle; several other nations, including Islamic consortiums and China, might use this tactic to begin vigorous expansion into space as soon as possible. American science and industry must maintain competitive positions, both in manned space efforts and in teleoperations and robotics.

With this fast-growing need for launch craft, we must develop vehicles beyond our excellent shuttles. With orbital transfer vehicles, SSTO cargo craft, and spaceplanes, we will have a solid foundation for commercial expansion to the Moon and elsewhere. If our military systems are made survivable to attack, attack is less likely. All launch systems for all future vehicles must be very much more practical than our current ones. We cannot become a spacefaring nation with only two launch sites.

Because an American GBMD is an urgent need, we propose to use our great strengths to achieve it. But we need a streamlined management team with innovative approaches; and we need to keep every advantage we possess, including our lead in microelectronics.

Critics of the Strategic Defense Initiative generally say either that we *can't* begin to build defenses now, or that we *shouldn't*. The first argument is technical, and requires examination. The second seems without merit: for the Soviet Union is already developing

strategic defenses. Their large radars demonstrate
that clearly.

If the Soviets can build strategic defenses, we can.
If they do—we *must*.

Legitimate Critics

Assured Survival has been opposed by the Bulletin
of the Atomic Scientists, the Federation of American
Scientists, the Union of Concerned Scientists, and
other such groups. This opposition is expected. They
have *always* opposed use of U.S. technology and military power to preserve U.S. national security. They
have *always* claimed that any escape from our present situation of danger is "provocative" and thus
impossible. They have *always* been more concerned
about the opinions of Soviet leaders than those of the
American people.

There are other critics whose voices must be
respected.

Chief among them are Freeman Dyson, of the Insti-
tute for Advanced Studies at Princeton, and Arthur
C. Clarke. Both have misgivings about the President's
Strategic Defense Initiative.

Freeman Dyson's book *Weapons and Hope* should
be required reading for anyone concerned with the
future of the strategic arms race. Dyson's analyses
are straightforward and often brilliant. He concludes
that MAD is immoral, and that some alternative must
be found.

Dyson summarizes his views as follows:

"1. I am in favor of strategic defense as a long-
range objective.

2. For various technical reasons, strategic defense
does not do well unless combined with arms control
applied to offensive weapons.

3. Likewise, drastic arms control of offensive weapons does not do well unless combined with strategic
defense.

4. Strategic defense and negotiated arms control

are not alternatives but must be pursued together in a balanced fashion."

There is little here for reasonable people to disagree with; but the analysis does not go far enough. What do we do if we cannot negotiate arms control of offensive weapons; or, having done so, we find that the Soviet Union is not keeping the agreement? Neither of these events is improbable. When asked what to do in those circumstances, Dyson's answer is "patience."

Dyson's argument—no strategic defense without arms control—has also been used by those who seek to put limits on the President's Strategic Defense Initiative: as we write this, the Congress has approved an amendment forbidding tests of satellite interceptor weapons unless the President certifies that he is seeking an agreement that would ban those weapons entirely. Mr. Dyson states that he is in agreement with those restrictions.

These views are not sound, for they give the Soviet Union a veto over testing and development of U.S. defense weapons.

A world in which strategic offensive weapons are limited by a verifiable treaty would be preferable to one with unlimited construction of such weapons. It is also unlikely. We should not reject the possibility, but we must not rely on arms control as our only hope.

If the Soviets will not agree to verifiable arms control of strategic offensive weapons, strategic defenses become even more important, and we must not shrink from a "defensive arms race."

Dyson rejects a strategy of "all out defense," as a "technological folly." The "folly," an all-consuming passion which overtakes an otherwise reasonable person, is more common in Britain than the United States. Doubtless a Ph.D. dissertation lurks in a study of precisely why this should be so. Since Dyson grew up in Britain, and was involved in the RAF during World War II, he is very concerned lest the U.S.

succumb to this common British malady. His "technical reasons" for rejecting defense without arms control are largely predicated on the theory that defenses cannot be made good enough: the aggressor will always be able to overwhelm them. Belief to the contrary is "technological folly."

Dyson's reasoning is largely drawn by analogy from a World War II device he helped to analyze: an automatic aiming device for bomber defense guns. Unfortunately, the automatic guns tended to shoot down far more British bombers than German fighters, because no automatic identification friend-or-foe (IFF) device could be made to work reliably. Nevertheless, high ranking RAF officers continued to pursue this "technological folly" and had not abandoned it at the end of the war.

Dyson sees strategic defense in much the same situation, and dismisses those who would put major U.S. effort into strategic defenses without arms control limitations of offensive weapons as victims of "technological folly." War, he says, is too horrible, and defenses are insufficiently reliable; we cannot place our trust in weapons alone.

The problem with all this is that Dyson's example is flawed. We could today build the World War II device which so eluded him in those years; and if we cannot construct a leak-proof defense system, we can certainly deploy systems effective enough to deter attack on us, and greatly to mitigate the effects of any attack that does take place. Governments have always tried to achieve this. Dyson, for all his technical wisdom, has fallen victim to the times: the stream of technological progress flows faster than we ever predict. (Science fiction writers have traditionally been the most "far out" in predicting technology: even the very best of those writing in the 40s, 50s, and even the 60's failed by a large margin to forsee advances in computer science that have already taken place.) The notion that the offense must be dominant is, today, nothing but a slogan; defensive weapons are not only feasible, but potentially decisive.

Dyson has forgotten Arthur C. Clarke's Law: "If a distinguished and grey-bearded scientist tells you that something is possible, believe him; if he says it is impossible, he is very probably wrong."

Arthur C. Clarke's objections are more narrowly technical. In his latest book *1984: SPRING* he argues that any space-based defense system must be vulnerable to the "bucket of nails" idiot attack: that is, an enemy simply launches a "bucket of nails" into an orbit exactly counter to the orbiting defense system. Sooner or later some of the nails will hit.

What both Clarke and Dyson failed to examine is the wide range of defensive systems available; and the highly stabilizing effects of *hardening* our space defenses. The "bucket of nails" can be formidable, but it can be countered; and the launching of such an attack is itself an act of warning. We have examined his other technical objections in the rest of this book.

Furthermore, the alternative to strategic defense is MAD; and MAD inevitably leads to launch on warning. Neither Dyson nor Clarke offer an escape from that other than the arms control willowisp—and both deplore launch on warning. At the very least, strategic defense will greatly lengthen the warning times available. That alone must be worth a very great deal. It may be worth everything.

What We Must Do

Our choices are clear. Adopting Assured Survival offers an arduous pathway toward making nuclear weapons obsolete and irrelevant. We may never reach that goal, but we would be going in the right direction.

Retaining the doctrine of MAD leads toward the scenario of the "War Games" film: computerized launch on warning. We may never reach that horrible situation, but that is where the road leads; we would be going in the wrong direction.

Assured Survival and a *defensive* arms race would at least stop the insanity of piling up more and more nuclear weapons. The "overkill" argument is specious:

no one accumulates weapons in order to "kill the other fellow ten times over," but rather to accomplish a specific mission: in our case, to have enough weapons survive an initial strike to be able to insure that the surviving remnant can assure the enemy's destruction. That is what "Assured Destruction" means, and it always implies an "overkill" capability. A *defensive* arms race accumulates weapons that, if used, harm only other weapons, not people.

Given mutual doctrines of Assured Survival— Mutual Assured Survival—we can envision a time when both the U.S. and the Soviet Union would find large strategic offensive forces too expensive to maintain, and could begin to scrap them, not because of agreements, but simply because they are not worth keeping: because they are obsolete and irrelevant.

Long before that time, the U.S. could opt for a targeting policy that spares Soviet citizens, and targets instead the repressive apparatus by which the Communist Party maintains its control of the U.S.S.R. For example: far from targeting Ukranian cities, the U.S. ought to target KGB headquarters, police stations, military garrisons; and ought to employ clean weapons, with as small a yield as possible. We do not want to kill Ukrainians. The more that survive, the more will be engaged in a war of national liberation against the Russians and Communists.

The "Minorities Question" terrifies the Soviet leadership even now. Proper targeting doctrine, and the development of the proper force structure, could add to those fears.

Defenses will never be good enough to let us begin a nuclear war in the expectation of winning it. A "win" which saw ten or twenty U.S. cities turned to blackened radioactive rubble would be an unprecedented disaster, and the leaders who brought that about would have to answer to the enraged survivors.

Yet: if the unthinkable happens; if, despite all our

efforts, a button is pushed: is it not better that 70% survive than that 90% (or more) die?

Mutual Assured Survival for all is a goal. It is a goal we may never entirely reach; but it is a goal worth striving for.

Acronyms

ABM	antiballistic missile
AI	artificial intelligence
BMD	ballistic missile defense (synonymous with DABM)
CEP	circular error probability
C^3I	command, control, communications, and intelligence
DoD	Department of Defense
DABM	defense against ballistic missiles (synonymous with BMD)
DARPA	Defense Advanced Research Projects Agency
ECM	electronic countermeasures
EHF	extremely high frequency
ELF	extremely low frequency
EMP	electromagnetic pulse
EMU	extravehicular mobility unit
FEL	free electron laser
FOBS	fractional orbital bombardment system
GBL	ground based laser
GBMD	global ballistic missile defense
GEO	geosynchronous Earth orbit
HAT	head aimed television
HEL	high energy laser
ICAO	International Congress of Aviation Organizations
ICBM	intercontinental ballistic missile
IOC	initial operational capability
IR	infrared
IRBM	intermediate range ballistic missile
JPL	Jet Propulsion Laboratory
LEO	low Earth orbit
LoADS	low altitude defense system
MAD	mutual assured destruction
MaRV	maneuverable reentry vehicle
MIRV	multiple independently-targetable reentry vehicle
MRBM	medium range ballistic missile

166

NRC	National Research Council
OAST	Office of Applications and Space Technology
PB	particle beam
RF	radio frequency
RMS	remote manipulator, shuttle
RV	reentry vehicle
SLBM	sea launched ballistic missile
SPS	solar power satellite
STC	space traffic control
UV	ultraviolet
VLF	very low frequency

APPENDICES

REPORT OF THE COMMITTEE ON STRATEGY

Military history teaches us that combined arms strategies have always been superior to single-weapons armies. Examples abound, ranging from Alexander the Great to World War II.

It is unlikely that any single system or approach will be adequate to the highly complex task of defending the United States against nuclear weapons and intercontinental ballistic missiles.

This Council recommends a multiple system approach to BMD and assured survival. In particular, we recommend:

- Multiple satellites using kinetic energy kill.
- Ground-based lasers with mirrors in space.
- Space-based lasers.
- Nuclear explosive-driven beam technologies collectively known as "third-generation systems."
- Ground-based point defense systems.

We also urge greatly accelerated research on the

many other candidate systems, such as particle beam weapons, which offer promise on the longer term.

This multiple-system approach to the defense of the nation offers the best possibility, because multiple defense systems can in part cover each other's vulnerabilities. A multiple system approach also forces any potential enemy to develop multiple attack systems. This diverts resources from his ability to attack U.S. citizens.

System Basing

Space-based systems have many inherent advantages over ground-based systems. The space system has a better field of view. There is no atmosphere to interfere with the kill mechanism. The space-based system can be closer to the target, and in any event the attack geometry is likely to be better. So-called pop-up ground systems, which rise to space before making their attack, overcome some of these disadvantages, but hardly all of them: their time for target acquisition and kill mechanism aiming is much shorter, and they must by definition rise from non-hostile territory—which is likely to be at some distance from the enemy's launch site.

Such systems, however, may be particularly valuable for defense against submarine-launched ballistic missiles fired close to U.S. shores, and indeed may be the best defense against such weapons.

Since ground-based pop-up systems are similar in nature to ICBMs, they are, of course, vulnerable to any boost-phase ICBM defense system, such as kinetic-energy kill systems of the High Frontier variety. The engagement becomes complex, but it is clear that these systems would be aided by the addition of other defensive weapons.

Space-based systems, and space-based components of ground-based systems, are desirable, but they are subject to a number of problems. Their key defect is vulnerability to attack in peacetime or in a wave attack at the beginning of the war.

The vulnerability of space-based systems is a severe problem. Their locations are known, and they can be attacked, sometimes with relatively crude weapons. One such attack is the proverbial "bucket of nails" thrown into the system's path. The space system's own velocity provides the kill mechanism.

Vulnerability

There are two overall approaches to the problem of space system vulnerabilities: active defense, and passive defense or hardening.

Active defense of space systems is inherently complex; the attack times are very short, so the active defense system must react quickly, generally during the boost phase if the attacking vehicle is a rocket. This can generate severe political problems. The "rules of engagement" for active defense of space weapons must be precisely defined, and either agreed to by both sides, or forced upon the other side.

None of this is impossible, but the problem is made easier when the system to be defended is hardened. Ideally, it should be sufficiently hardened to require a direct hit or near miss by a nuclear weapon, which would give unambiguous warning of impending attack against the U.S. Strategic Offensive Forces.

That kind of hardening isn't easy to come by.

However, space systems *can* be hardened. Protective shields, built in layers, can be deployed. Note that shields need not surround the system.

One design for such shields consists of alternate layers of hard materials, such as concrete, and absorptive materials (sometimes called "shaving cream" because that is what is often used in ballistic laboratories).

Neither concrete nor shaving cream is light in weight.

Hardening Materials

Hardening can be quite effective, but it is also costly. There seems to be no general agreement on the price of a pound put into orbit, but it isn't low.

Getting a lot of materials into orbit won't be cheap.

The best method for doing it depends on what methods we have available—and on how much material we want to put into orbit.

There are three general ways we might put hardening materials into Earth orbit. They are:

• Incremental approach: more Shuttles, and perhaps improved expendable rockets.
• Heavy Lift Vehicle.
• Extra-terrestrial materials.

The cost effectiveness of these approaches depends in large part on *how much* material one wants in orbit. If we only want to harden a few satellites, shuttles and expendables will do the job. If we want to harden more, we would do better to construct a new recoverable Heavy Lift Vehicle. If we want to harden a lot of them, and make them very hard, we will need extra-terrestrial materials.

However, reliance on the incremental approach alone is likely to result in "too little and too late." The United States at present faces a severe shortfall in capability to put materials into orbit. This is true whether we consider military or civilian requirements.

It is vital that we increase our capability to place mass in orbit. It is likely that *all* of the above approaches will be necessary.

Heavy Lift Vehicle

A fleet of Heavy Lift Vehicles would cost between $5 and $20 billion. Given Presidential priority, it could be built in fewer than six years. Once built, the cost of hardening materials would be low.

Such a fleet would ensure the U.S. position in space for the foreseeable future. Large projects, such as Solar Power Satellites to deliver power to ourselves, our allies, and developing countries, might become feasible.

A permanent manned space station would be inevitable and almost trivially easy, as would a program of peaceful scientific exploration of the Moon and planets. Industrial exploitation of space would be greatly simplified.

The credibility of our space defense systems would be raised considerably, because we would have demonstrated our capability to operate in space, and we would have a large pool of trained talent to draw upon.

Extra-terrestrial Materials

The capability to capture extra-terrestrial materials in large quantities would have many of the same effects as the construction of a Heavy Lift Vehicle Fleet. Many of the economic advantages would also accrue; for example, the construction of lunar-based solar power stations capable of beaming power to the Earth (and to other space operational facilities).

Constructing a fleet of Heavy Lift Vehicles would make possible the acquisition of extra-terrestrial materials, but is not necessary for the task.

There are two possible sources for extra-terrestrial materials in large quantities:

- Asteroid recovery.
- Lunar materials.

Both these methods should be pursued; however, the lunar base option seems more feasible, given present capabilities and technologies.

Uses of the Moon in Defense

Extra-terrestrial materials certainly make construction and hardening of space-based components for BMD much simpler and cheaper. The capability also promises a direct economic return. Given intelligent planning, we can make the defense program pay for itself through the development of new technologies. We will also benefit from any resources recovered from the Moon. Although lunar manufacturing is not likely to be economically important in this century, it will certainly become so as the next century begins.

Several of the systems recommended by this Council require space-based components. Whatever defensive systems are adopted, the long-term and permanent defense of the U.S. (going well beyond the year 2000) will certainly require space-based components of a BMD system, and this probably means using extra-terrestrial materials. "Green cheese"—i.e., lunar materials—is acceptable, and its use in the long term is probably inevitable.

The sooner we reestablish lunar operations, the quicker and cheaper we can have survivable components of BMD. Naturally the costs are not low. On the other hand, they aren't excessive. A permanent lunar base, with the ability to deliver quantities of lunar material into Earth orbit, could be constructed in about ten years at an average cost of about $10 billion (1983) per year. Adjusted for inflation this is about the cost of Project Apollo.

Note that Apollo had many economic advantages, including stimulation of high-tech research and development; many of our economic woes did not come until our retreat from space.

Any long-term defense system requires mass and fuel. Both are obtainable from lunar materials.

Mass is required for hardening and shielding. As potential enemy capabilities inevitably increase, more mass will be required to shield defense satellites. Although all this could be supplied from Earth, there comes a point at which it is much cheaper (even with the initial development costs) to supply it from the Moon.

A lunar installation has another great advantage: it provides a hardened Command and Control center, similar to the "Citadel" basing concept proposed for Peacekeeper. Vulnerability of the U.S. Command, Control, Communications, and Intelligence capabilities is one of the key problems of U.S. defense.

Manned Systems
Another approach to the problem of vulnerability is to place U.S. officers aboard defensive satellites.

This considerably raises the psychological threshold of attack on these systems.

There are obvious Command, Control, and Communications advantages to this approach. Reliability and credibility of observation is greatly increased. If, during the transition between MAD and Assured Survival, it becomes necessary temporarily to adopt a policy of Launch On Early Warning, reliable observation of an attack becomes vital.

One system proposes approximately 400 stations, each with a crew of 3 to 5. Any single such "frontier post" would be highly vulnerable to attack, but it would be very difficult to destroy all of them, and impossible to do so in secrecy.

It is likely that any early defense system will require manned components, if only for inspection, maintenance, assembly, and checkout.

The *Skylab* experience has demonstrated that we have the technology to keep crews in space for the requisite times.

We therefore offer the following conclusions and recommendations.

1. We recommend an immediate program for lunar and asteroidal exploration. This need not be extensive, but there should be a lunar polar satellite to determine whether or not there is water ice at the lunar poles; and an asteroidal probe to gain new knowledge about these critical bodies.

2. We note that the civilian space program has a direct impact on the nation's capability for defense. A lunar base makes certain space defense systems much cheaper and simpler to build and operate.

3. The United States at present faces a severe shortfall in capability to place systems in orbit. We must *immediately* undertake programs to increase our lift capability.

4. Military operations must be routine. Defense of

the United States will require personnel experienced in space operations.

5. We believe that an extensive civil space program can be justified on its own merits; a commitment to a strategy of assured survival and defense makes such a program imperative. The civil space program provides a pool of experienced talent and capabilities, precisely as a civil aviation program feeds military aviation.

CO-VENTURING

The ultimate (and perhaps most important) benefit of an expanded military program in space will be
the joint applications of the new technology. These
could create entirely new industries on Earth as well
as in space, with increased employment and a higher
economic profile for the nation as a whole. Civilian
space programs have already enhanced existing technologies and created new ones; a military program
will certainly do likewise, in a number of ways. The
technologies developed in one program will be useful
to the other.

A renewed space program will also have profound
effects on our education system, just as a strategy of
Assured Survival will give new hope to the nation.

Historical Examples

Many non-military products and techniques the
twentieth-century American takes for granted have
come from military research and development. This
is especially true in the transportation field. The
United States entered World War I woefully un-
prepared; there were few airplanes in the military
services and even fewer in private hands. American

industry produced not one single warplane during
World War I.

Now, everywhere in the world, whoever flies speaks
English. When Soviet pilots were airlifting supplies
into Cairo, Egypt, during the Yom Kippur War, both
the Soviet pilots and the Egyptian air traffic controllers spoke to one another in English over the radio
because this was the one language that both understood! The same strange communication goes on today in English between Soviet pilots and Cuban air
traffic controllers in the Caribbean. It all derives
from the enormous pre-eminence of American aircraft,
pilots, and support facilities in place immediately
following World War II, as a result of military emphasis on air transport.

This dramatic change in world leadership took place
in part because Congress recognized the problem
and established the National Advisory Committee on
Aeronautics (NACA). Many of the aeronautical engineering advances developed by NACA were later employed in the world-famous Douglas airliners which
revolutionized air travel in the United States; the
NACA technology used in the DC-3 included radial
engine cowlings that improved cooling while at the
same time reducing drag.

Many of today's general aviation aircraft utilize
NACA technology developed during World War II—
laminar flow airfoils, for example.

American pre-eminence in international air transport can be traced to the development of the Douglas
C-54 four-engined aircraft which, in the hands of
USAAF pilots and airline contract pilots, blazed the
transoceanic air routes of the world. As a result, the
C-54 became the first of the post-war air transports,
the DC-4, which grew into the DC-6 and DC-7 aircraft which in turn continued to give the American
aeronautical industry and the airlines world pre-
eminence.

Although the Boeing 707 was originally designed

as a commercial jet airliner, the Air Force purchase of the aircraft as the KC-153 tanker assisted Boeing in amortizing the development of the 707. Military development of jet engines showed its civilian utility in the 707's jet engines which, in turn, were used on the Douglas DC-8. The wide-bodied airliners of today came about as a result of an Air Force requirement for a heavy-lift military transport aircraft. Three American aerospace firms bid for this large contract—Douglas, Lockheed, and Boeing. When Lockheed won the contract, Boeing used their CX design expertise to come up with the 747. Douglas in turn used their experience to develop the DC-10. The high-bypass turbofan engines used on these airliners came directly from the development of their military counterparts for the CX program.

There were technological advances in aviation due to military support of R&D as well as to military hardware developments. The *cost* of air transportation has likewise dropped because military RDT&E paid for the technology. Benefits were directly transplanted to civilian and commercial use without an enormous burden of capital investment in RDT&E, which would have had to be subsequently amortized out of the civilian pocket. This has made a great deal of high technology both available *and* affordable in the civilian sector.

POTENTIAL CIVILIAN USE OF
MILITARY SPACE ACTIVITIES

Military and civilian technologies fade into each other because technology itself is merely applied science.

We cannot predict all of the advances that will be generated by the creation of space stations, lunar colonies and planetoid mining. The achievements themselves will be awesome; what we learn from them will lead to further achievements.

Some things can be predicted.

Focusing specifically on a Ballistic Missile Defense (BMD) system, the advances will come not only in space, but in earth-based computer technology. The need for supercomputers to coordinate and aim BMD lasers goes beyond current achievements; what will begin as classified military supercomputers and their programs will ultimately influence civilian computers, advancing the state of the art much more rapidly. The DOD will commission civilian firms to create these systems, also expanding employment and encouraging higher education in the computer sciences.

Any form of laser BMD will have the side effect of telling us how to build the more advanced laser

183

systems needed for "Laser launched cargo rockets."
One approach is to fire into a rocket nozzle; the
exhaust gas would be superheated air or vaporized
rocket nozzle wall; the exhaust velocity would be
tremendous. Cost of launching payloads to orbit would
drop to dollars per pound. The lasers needed are
three orders of magnitude more powerful than those
required to destroy incoming missiles, but the BMD
lasers would inevitably serve as prototypes.

Cargo vehicles lift anything. The present Shuttle,
though operated by the civilian component of our
space program, NASA, also serves the military. Spacecraft designed for military use will also lift civilian
cargos, even before the spacecraft becomes militarily
obsolete.

Nuclear bombs came before nuclear power plants.
Computer programs designed to pinpoint a rising
enemy missile will pinpoint other things: the exact
location of a civilian airliner or a lost Boy Scout.
Military spy satellites are mapping the Earth even
now; *anyone* can use a better map. Military navigation satellites (Navstar) have been used to steer a
civilian jet liner on a transatlantic flight from the
United States to France with a final accuracy of
about 25 feet at the end of the flight.

The High Frontier concept will require that we
learn how to assemble machinery and habitats in
space. Civilian projects need these capabilities too.
We will develop them together. Civilian and military
groups among our forefathers worked together to
conquer a hostile environment, the Great Wilderness,
which in many respects was far more dangerous than
space has turned out to be in our time.

Implications For Space Science Activities

Scientific circles tend to believe that the funding
pie is finite and that they must compete for even a
small slice. What is not well understood is that an
increased military involvement in space means a
larger pie. It also means improved technology at a

lower cost. Lower costs will in turn permit an increased level of space science activity.

There will be more flight opportunities available, lower launching costs, a broader variety of launch vehicles and deep space vessels, the ability of scientists to accompany critical in-space experiments, and one or more manned space stations that can also be used for scientific research. Lunar and planetary missions launched from a manned space station in low-Earth orbit (LEO) will benefit from the same rationale that currently exists with commercial satellites launched from the shuttle orbiter: an opportunity to build, check-out, and launch these unmanned probes from space under the watchful eyes of the project scientists themselves.

If any military system in space requires massive solid shielding against attack, most of this mass will be obtained from the Moon. Regular manned flights to the Moon will be made again, this time on a more permanent basis with scientists accompanying them.

Going to the planetoid belt to get mass shielding would mean that we can also send scientists to Mars, Jupiter, and eventually the other Outer Planets. This capability implies the development of the necessary closed-cycle life support systems, which in turn means that people can live in space anywhere they wish as long as they wish.

The development of any teleoperator technology in conjunction with the deployment of a ballistic missile defense system also offers opportunities for the application of this technology to unmanned scientific missions. (Scientists *really* began to explore the continent of Antarctica once the U.S. Navy was capable of supporting exploration of that continent in the late 1950's in conjunction with the naval requirement for weather and hydrographic data obtainable on the southern polar continent.)

The **rediscovery of progress** is a reasonable goal for the United States in the 1980's. Progress is possible. We do not have to accept limits to growth.

The most underestimated and least mentioned benefit of the development of space resources is to capture the imagination of the American people and to motivate our youth. A renewed space program—military or civilian—will have an enormous impact on our technical education system, drawing bright young people into technical careers. This will have great and beneficial impact for many years to come.

There is enormous potential benefit from developing space resources. By acquiring new technologies and expanding the U.S. resource base, we can make the defense program pay for itself.

STABILITY

One of the major objections to changing from Mutual Assured Destruction (MAD) to Mutual Assured Survival has been the fear that there might be a period of instability, during which the Soviet Union might have a high incentive to launch a pre-emptive first strike.

The motive for this pre-emptive war would be the fear that once the United States achieves a defensive capability, we might then be tempted to attack the Soviet Union, since we could presumably do so with impunity.

This would imply a defense system which was perceived to be nearly leakproof. That kind of technology is unlikely. However, the issue remains important. The following signed papers address the issue.

THE STABILITY OF ASSURED SURVIVAL

Stefan T. Possony and J. E. Pournelle

Long Term Stability

The alternative to Assured Survival is continued reliance on Mutual Assured Destruction, or MAD. The MAD doctrine requires invulnerable weapons.

Weapons may be made "invulnerable" through their basing, or through doctrine. We know of no basing scheme that guarantees survival of the Strategic Offensive Forces (SOF) past the end of this decade. Survival of the SOF must increasingly depend on active measures.

There are two classes of active measures. One, defensive systems, is here recommended. The alternative is one or another form of offensive protection: preventive war, pre-emptive strike, or launch on early warning.

A ballistic missile defense (BMD) system need not be perfect or "leak-proof" in order to increase global security. A large part of the strategy of Assured Survival depends upon complicating any potential enemy's war plan. An enemy planner contemplating

189

attack on the U.S. cannot know which of his weapons will penetrate, and which U.S. offensive weapons will survive. As his uncertainty of success increases, his incentive to launch an attack decreases.

This situation is symmetrical if both sides possess BMD systems. If only one side has BMD, the situation is more complex; however, unless the BMD system is considerably more effective than any system we can foresee in the near future, the United States would have little incentive to launch a first strike. BMD systems provide much more protection for missiles and weapons than for cities. A 75% interception of incoming warheads would be more than adequate to protect a missile farm, but hardly acceptable for protecting our citizens. Precisely what level of destruction to U.S. cities is unacceptable may be debated, but surely no elected official will risk the destruction of even one, much less several, of our major cities. Note also that there is no way to know which cities will survive and which will be destroyed.

Furthermore, U.S. resources invested in defense systems have not been invested in offensive systems. The argument that BMD is part of a first strike falls to the ground in the absence of a major and massive program of offensive weapon construction.

Our present plans call for increasing the SOF by addition of some 50 Peacekeeper missiles. Fifty Peacekeepers would not be a counterforce capability against the Soviet Union. They are a significant counterforce with respect to any *other* nation. Since the U.S. has always held significant strategic superiority with respect to the rest of the world, this is hardly a change in world stablility.

Short Term Instabilities

It is possible that during the construction of a ballistic missile defense system, the Soviet Union will believe that it has a temporary capability to disarm the United States at acceptable cost; and that this capability will vanish once the U.S. has deployed defensive weapons.

It can be argued that a sufficiently aggressive Soviet leadership might be tempted to launch preventive war under those circumstances.

Our defensive strategy may be threatened by the Soviets maximizing their terror impacts and relying on straightforward threats backed up by their superiority in throw weight, and perhaps laser technologies. They may be tempted to believe that the American people will give in and abort the defensive effort. Under no circumstances will the United States protect our strategic weapons from being destroyed in a surprise attack.

Given vulnerable weapon systems and no strategic defenses, there is little alternative to a policy of launching on warning. This is not a good strategy, but lacking something better—and absent deployed defensive systems we do not see a better—then we have no choice but to employ a second-rate strategy.

If the Soviets should threaten us to prevent new deployments—as they do with the Pershing II—then the only feasible alternative, launch-on-warning, must be spelled out to them. Any doctrine of launch on warning is, in our judgment, less stable than a policy based on defense; but absent defense, the increasing vulnerability of the Strategic Offensive Forces moves us inexorably toward launch-on-warning as the only possible salvation to Mutual Assured Destruction.

A policy of Assured Survival, based on effective active defense systems, allows much greater variation in global tensions, since accidents are less likely to trigger a full-scale launch.

A policy of Mutual Assured Survival allows both sides to live without the constant threat of nuclear annihilation. It obviously offers more long-term stability than MAD.

BALLISTIC MISSILE DEFENSE AND ARMS CONTROL

Lt. Gen. Daniel O. Graham, USA (Ret.)

A vigorous U.S. effort to emplace a non-nuclear defense against ballistic missiles should be viewed as encouraging, not detrimental to arms control efforts. To date, arms control efforts have been constrained by the all-offense Mutual Assured Destruction policy to seek "balance" in the balance of terror. Such efforts have not been marked by success.

So long as long-range strategic missiles are deemed essential to the military policies of both sides—an inexorable element in the MAD context—there is little chance of viable agreements. However, once the value of such weapons is diminished by effective defenses, the urge to add more of them or to retain them in current numbers will abate.

The thrust for Assured Survival in technical terms should be coupled with a new thrust in U.S. Arms Control efforts. The Soviets should be approached with a view to achieving an agreement that both sides may deploy defense-only systems, non-nuclear with inspection safeguards. Such a political effort must proceed concurrently with the U.S. defensive system development and acquisition. However, U.S. acquisition of a defensive system should not be conditional on success in this effort.

There is an enormously different effect between the acquisition of an effective space-control system on the part of the United States and the acquisition of similar capabilities by the Soviet Union.

If the United States deploys a space-based defense against long-range ballistic missiles, there can be no doubt that we would permit the Soviets to acquire similar capabilities and to pursue other space goals to support peaceful endeavors.

It is by no means certain, probably unlikely, that the Soviets would allow the United States such free entry to space should they first acquire a capability to intercept space-bound missiles and other boosters with other missions.

The Soviets are, in fact, already engaged in an effort to secure military control of space. They have the only space weapons now extant. Further, the evidence available indicates a broad-front, well-funded Soviet effort to achieve military dominance of near-Earth space. However, the Soviets know full well that the United States has fundamental technical advantages over them in space technology. They therefore press for treaties which would deny us the option of countering their offensive capabilities with space-borne defenses.

*   *   *

THOUGHTS ON STABILITY

Arthur Kantrowitz, Ph.D.
Dartmouth College

Some Americans, but not many Russians, assert that any attempt to exit MAD via defense increases our danger by destabilizing the present standoff.

Let's start from the strong point that gives us some

faith in the stability of MAD . . . we have some knowledge of what goes on in the USSR largely from observation satellites. Without this knowledge, MAD would be completely unstable to self-excited rumors. Secondly, let us remember the wisdom of Madariaga who pointed out that, "Nations don't distrust each other because they are armed; they are armed because they distrust each other."

These statements provide an essential clue to the proper escape from MAD. The way out is to increase knowledge of each others's activities, which will reduce the distrust driving the arms race. The way out is reduction of secrecy—the extension of openness to the world.

Open societies have evolved in an international jungle. What is the source of the survival strength of Open societies? Openness is the antidote, perhaps the only antidote, to corruption. Those of us who have had experience with military secrecy know very well how often it is abused for interservice rivalries, for partisan purposes, for the concealment of official blunders, for concealment of the many abuses of government power. Secrecy conceals corruption which, in time, destroys the strength of any society.

But, you may respond, there is also strength in secrecy, the power of surprise in military tactics, etc. However, it is easy to distinguish between such short time applications of secrecy which cannot conceal corruption for very long.

Imagine now a world in which secrecy had been drastically reduced. The opportunities to use the space-based weapons President Reagan spoke of in his March 23 speech to accomplish his escape from MAD are now delightfully plentiful. Openness and only openness can make the defenses we build against ballistic missiles symmetrical and thus not destabilizing. MAD has been stabilized by the openness produced by reconnaissance satellites. We can escape from it by more openness.

I would like to point out that the Reagan administration has recently been tightening secrecy and worrying more about the transfer of technology to the Soviet Union. I am persuaded that this policy will make the escape from MAD more difficult. I believe this penny-wise pound-foolish secrecy tightening to be inconsistent with the magnificent challenge to escape MAD that the President has offered us. He should make up his mind which he wants.

*   *   *

BALLISTIC MISSILE DEFENSE AS A STABILIZING FORCE

Gregory Benford, Ph.D.
University of California at Irvine

The primary opposition to the BMD idea will NOT come from those who view total disarmament as the only solution to our problem.

Instead, the bulk of the American people and the Congress will assess the BMD concept for its impact on *stability* of our deterrent. Here we can make valuable points.

1. BMD can prevent accidents—which many consider the most probable way a nuclear war can start. Properly designed, a VERY LIMITED deployment will allow us to knock down a few, accidentally launched warheads.

2. BMD can be supplemented by arms negotiations which do not require difficult weapons reductions. We can set up routine methods to exchange launch timetables. Launches outside a given time window can be considered accidents, and knocked down. This provides a method of clear accident identification and virtually automatic defense. This makes even a small BMD deployment highly stabilizing.

3. BMD adds a new, difficult-to-assess element to the strategic equation. Uncertainty about ability to launch a surgical first strike is stabilizing, as long as neither side believes a major assault can be totally

stopped. (This last scenario will never occur. No plausible scenario will yield one power with an absolute shield and the other with nothing.)

These points should disarm many of BMD's critics. They demonstrate that Mutual Assured Survival is squarely on the side of stability, using a deterrent *which threatens no noncombatants*. We will pre-empt many opponents.

POLITICAL FACTORS AND PERSUASION

Chairman's note: The Citizens Advisory Council is largely formed from experts in space science and technology. However, it also includes students, homemakers, and others. Greg Bear is a young writer invited to attend by the Chairman of the Council. His paper speaks directly to the problem of public persuasion.

CONVERSION

By Greg Bear

Before I attended the recent conference of the Citizens Advisory Council on National Space Policy, I firmly believed in a purely civilian space effort. I felt uneasy about additional military spending for strategic weapon systems, which did not seem to provide any greater security, but simply took us one step farther down the road to nuclear disaster. In short, I held the attitudes of many educated moderate liberals in the world today—sticking to ideals which define the United States as a nation of independent civilians, served by the military, and not vice versa.

I still hold these attitudes. But I am now ready to put aside my feelings about increased military expenditures and a greater military role in space. An alternative to the most foolish and dangerous strategic policy in our time has been suggested, and it is a sound alternative. It will involve expenditures equal to or greater than the amounts being spent on bigger and better offensive weapons today. It will guarantee the military a major role in space (something which was inevitable anyway). But it may also lead us away from nuclear holocaust, and away from the policy of Mutual Assured Destruction (MAD).

For decades, the Department of Defense has been unable to defend the United States against nuclear attack. Mutual Assured Destruction was adopted as the major strategic policy simply because there *was* no way to prevent warheads from destroying much of the United States. Weapons were built and stockpiled which could be described as "defensive" only by incredible twists of logic. These hugely destructive "weapons of peace" could, in turn, be countered only by similar armaments.

The upward spiral of MAD, of defenseless Defense and overkill Offense, created the world in which I grew up. Generations have now lived with the prospect of seeing the end of civilization on Earth— perhaps the end of life itself. How this has shaped the psychology of nations, much less individuals, is of concern in itself; but the prospect of Armageddon is incontrovertible reality. We may not be able to completely imagine it, but we know it is possible. Many believe it is inevitable. Until now, I could bring up only vague and unsupported arguments to counter those who maintain our days are numbered.

To change this horrible status quo, I am willing to modify my ideals. I believe that millions of Americans with similar beliefs will support a far-reaching shift in national defense policy, even should it be more expensive.

The key is that the spending must truly be for *defense*. MAD is outmoded because we now have the means to prevent nuclear missiles from landing on our cities. Since the development of nuclear weapons and MAD, technologies heretofore found only in science fiction have matured into reality. Powerful lasers already have military applications; Particle-Beam weapons have been developed in the last decade which may ultimately prove more effective than lasers. And with our increased achievement and flexibility in spaceflight, we can now place these systems where they will be most effective: in orbit.

From orbit, or even on the surface of the moon, lasers and other weapons will be useless as weapons of mass destruction. They are effective only in high-energy bursts directed at specific small targets. In other words, they are ideal for point-by-point destruction of offensive weapons such as missiles.

The expert technical consultants to the Citizens Advisory Council on National Space Policy have agreed that such systems are feasible, and could be in place by 1990. If strategic defense becomes national policy, then by 2000, or 2010, our defenses may be sufficient to "knock down" a large percentage of any first strike. Total nuclear destruction may become a nightmare of the past.

By building these systems, we do not eliminate the threat of war. We reduce the likelihood of war; this cannot be said for military spending to support the MAD policy currently in force.

Doubtless the deployment of defensive anti-missile systems in space will lead to a race between the nuclear superpowers. But the focus of the race will be away from the destruction of cities and nations; the focus will be on the creation and protection of defense systems *in space*. If a war must be fought, space is a far better location than Earth.

There are additional benefits. In the past, the military has developed frontiers originally pioneered by civilians. In time, military development has led to more civilian involvement, and in some instances whole new industries have grown up. Air transportation and oceanographic exploration come to mind immediately. Systems created for the military, such as radar and sonar, have become indispensable in our high-technology world. Increased military presence in space will require space transportation systems which will inevitably be used by civilians as well.

My greatest dream is to see humans expanding into space. It has been said—by the Russian space pioneer Tsiolkovsky—that Earth is indeed the cradle of mankind, but that no one can remain in the cradle forever.

With the systems proposed by the High Frontier group, we can protect the cradle of the Earth, and we can begin to lift ourselves into our next frontier. We must survive into adulthood, and inevitably that adulthood will be spent in space.

The Independence of America:
Towards a New Beginning

By Robert W. Bussard, Ph.D.

President, INESCO. Former Director of Fusion Energy Project, Los Alamos National Laboratories.

Over two hundred years ago the brilliant and dedicated men who founded our country lighted a light never before seen on the planet; the light of freedom for a new society and for its individual people, beyond the oppressive bounds of foreign influence, laws, and domination. Their struggle took twelve years from its formal beginnings in 1776 until its conclusion with the adoption of the United States Constitution in 1788. That twelve years was a time of trial for our country, with contending factions arguing for differing socio-economic models of "freedom" for the citizens of their several independent States and Commonwealths—which had not long before been the thirteen Colonies of England and King George III. Freedom for society and man was a new idea and, like all new ideas, was interpreted in different ways by different people. The general consensus that was reached by 1788 was sufficient to allow the adoption of our Constitution, which endures to the present day.

These Founders of our country, Franklin, Jefferson, Adams, Washington, and all the others, were drawn together by a commonality of despair. They had all become men driven to action by the steady erosion of the rights of free men under the oppressive policies of the English government. This erosion and suppression of the rights of free Englishmen under the Crown had gone on for over twenty years before the final break in 1776, as a conscious policy of the King and his minions in Parliament. Individual liberties of the free colonists had been legislated away, and oppressive policies constraining trade and taxation had been imposed one-by-one, until their burden was too great to bear. As late as 1774 the government of the several Colonies petitioned King George III to restore their rights as free Englishmen— to no avail. And all attempts by the Colonists to render illegal and thus halt the trade in slaves were stopped by action of the Crown, thus ensuring the basis for the great Civil War which was to grip the country only seventy-two years after its final establishment as a coherent nation.

For over twenty years the citizens of America suffered under harmful tariffs on trade, unfair taxation of domestic and imported goods, and progressive denial of rights of dissent, free speech, control of arms for individual and collective safety (against the sometimes hostile Indians and French), prohibition of emancipation of slaves and a host of other freedoms we now take for granted.

Driven to despair, but full of desire and hope for the new nation they could sense emerging on this continent, our Founders placed their worldly goods, their very lives, and—as they said—their "sacred honor" on the block when they took that first, awful, terrifying step of declaring themselves and their colonies to be free and independent of foreign domination and control.

The Current Predicament
Today we face a situation which is in some ways

very similar to that confronting the delegates in Independence Hall in the Summer of 1776. We have witnessed a progressive erosion of our ability to act in the best interests of our nation by more than twenty years of accommodation to international pressures and "world opinion," as these have been described to us by politicians and the public media, yearning to accommodate in order to avoid confrontation with our enemies, the enemies of our kind of free society. For decades we have surrendered, a mile at a time, the hard won ground of liberty and its defense, to a hostile world in which governments based on collectivism—not individual freedom—have sworn to "bury" us and all that we are and for which we stand.

It has taken more than twenty years to bring us to this state; a state where the strength of strategic weapons in the hands of the Soviet Union far exceeds our own, where our navies are challenged and matched upon the seas, and our armies (including those of our allies) are far over-matched on the ground. We have let it all gradually slip away, almost unnoticed, by policies of "detente," willingness to accept "parity/equality" in the nuclear balance of terror, acceptance of SALT talks and treaties which have led to the growing strength of our foes and the gradual weakening of ourselves.

Creeping up on us in the dark of night of murky international politics, and sometimes with our own well-meaning but misguided policies, has been the dragon of despair—despair at the shackles we have let be placed on our abilities to act—the same kind of despair and frustration that grasped our nation's Founders in 1774–75. There is nothing wrong with the people of America—we are still tough and independent souls who, in the large, cherish our freedoms and despise unwarranted constraints; who want safe homes and firesides, and who are willing to fight for them if we know they are endangered and if we are given the chance to do so.

The Threat Is Very Real

Yes, Virginia, there really is an enemy. It is that political force loose in the world which places governments above people, conformity to the State above individual liberty, rigidity of thought above freedom of expression. This force finds it greatest and most threatening embodiment in those nations espousing "communism," and whose governments operate dictatorially on models of State planning in which individuals are "workers," not free citizens.

An organized dictatorship is an efficient form of government—in its ability to exploit and build on human and other national resources—but it is not a free one. Independence of spirit and of the mind is not a valued national asset in such societies. For this reason alone a free society will always prevail in the long run of things—provided it can stay alive to do so.

Staying alive in the jungle of the world does not happen by agreeing with our enemies. Their interests are **theirs,** not ours. Staying alive requires that we hold fast to all of our principles and stand firmly on the grounds of the rights of free men to remain free, as did the farmers at Concord Bridge so long ago. The first five American war dead are buried under a small monument on Lexington Green. They died never knowing whether their cause would triumph, but believing it essential **not** to agree to accommodate to the King's soldiers.

We now face a world of media, politicians, and minority agitation groups which wants us to accommodate still more to cries of "peace," "detente," "coexistence" and all the other claptrap of left-wing communist favoritism which seeks "peace in our time—at almost any price." Who are they to tell us what to do? Are we not capable of deciding what is best for **us,** for our nation and our people, ourselves? Why should we accommodate to further demands not to build those military weapons we really do need for our defense? Indeed, the time is long past for us to look to *our own* safety and *our own* weapons to guarantee that safety—*no one else and no other nation will do so for us.*

The size of the threat is quite frightening when it is viewed fully and in the light of a clear day, not befogged by intellectualisms and the protocols of international political debate. Any one of us knows a gun held to our head when we see it—all we have to do is see it. And that is what has been so carefully "talked over" and concealed by all the words of the intellectual media/minority rhetoric—the size and number of the "guns" which threaten us. Indeed these threatening developments by our enemies, which have brought us to this point of danger, have almost never been clear and obvious to us, but have come to our awareness year after year, a bit at a time. A new Soviet thermonuclear bomb test, a new Russian ICBM development, a new and faster nuclear submarine, a succession of nuclear reactor space satellites for intelligence data-gathering, beam weapon development for ABM use, massive chemical and biological attack systems, and on and on.

Year after year Soviet developments have step-by-step increased their ability to destroy American defenses and American cities. Year after year our analysts and policymakers have tried to view each new step as a Soviet effort to reach a "stable" military balance with our own forces, following our own doctrine of Mutual Assured Destruction (MAD), which we have clung to for thirty years. And year after year the media establishment has portrayed such developments as peace-keeping *in intent* for the long run, and has tried to convince us all that things are *not* so bad, that the balance of terror is moving in the "right" direction and that the Soviet's intentions are—and must of necessity be—peaceful.

So we are here now, facing a Soviet arsenal of five more ICBM systems than have we, with over three times our nuclear weapons delivery capacity, a Soviet fleet that outranks our own in those kinds of ships which will matter most in any future conflict, Soviet aircraft at least as fast and maneuverable as our own, a nuclear weapons arsenal broader in scope than ours and far greater than needed to destroy America, and—most importantly—a never wavering commitment to acquiring the high ground of Space.

Unlike our space program, which took a "one-shot" goal of lunar landing and then died as the Viet Nam war engulfed us, to be revitalized a decade later by the beautiful Shuttle, the Soviets have kept up an unrelenting launch rate into orbit, with ever increasing launches and payloads. They have been occupying a manned space station now for over four years, and it has been made larger over that time by further assembly in space. Their array of communications, navigation, and spy satellites matches our own. Their work on high power lasers, special nuclear weapons, particle beams, and high power microwave tubes started years before our own, and has been and is pursued with great vigor and at great cost—aimed at the eventual development of defensive weapons systems to render our counter-forces ineffective. As this happens—and it is happening now—our MAD doctrine of survival by continued balance-of-terror will fail in a cataclysmic way and we will be left without provision for "the common defense" of our nation and our people, unless we take immediate steps to mobilize America and American industry and ingenuity to build true defensive systems. We must put new guns over our fireplaces, else our homes and our land become hopeless hostages to the evil forces arrayed against us.

The Soviets are not nine feet tall—they are no better than we at such things and are, in fact, far worse in some respects because of the immense burden of their governmental bureaucracy. But they are dedicated, committed, and continue to put huge resources of people and money into their national military machine. Khrushchev's boast so long ago that "we will bury you" is no idle threat, no political rhetoric. He was speaking from his knowledge of what they really were—and are—doing to overwhelm our ability to defend ourselves, and to protect our country and ourselves, our families and our homes.

Our Failures Lie With Our Selves

That our enemies have been able to reach a commanding and growing advantage over us is no accident. It is a product of Soviet drive and initiative to build ever stronger aggressive offensive military forces, coupled with major efforts by Soviet disinformation and propaganda mills to lead us into a false sense of security under which we would not do—and so far have not done—those things needed to assure our long-term survival. In this latter effort they have had the helping hands on our side of a succession of American governments who failed to tell our people of each new escalation in the threat, who often-times did not wish, even in the face of measured facts, to admit the existence of such threats, and the help of the press and the TV media which has propagandized us for decades to think that the Soviet's intentions are or must surely be peaceful, like our own, and that they—like us—only wish to live in "peaceful co-existence."

With such views, who could hold beliefs that they might be engaged in massive military developments of country-killing weapons systems when such systems clearly do not fit the needs of "peaceful co-existence." It has thus been argued that these developments must be misunderstood, or be for other purposes (defense against the Chinese), or possibly exaggerated or even non-existent. *None of the above is true.* Unfortunately, the lack of candor of our past governments and the proselytizing propaganda of the media have led many of our honest citizens to believe that things will all come out right in the end, because everyone's intentions are honorable—we have begun to drink this nonsense that the Soviet propagandists have been trying to sell us in the west.

In this complex interaction of facts, analysis, propaganda, and belief we have helped the cause of our enemies immensely by a continuing almost blind adherence to a national doctrine for strategic survival that was invented and adopted over twenty-five years ago. This is the doctrine of Mutual Assured Destruction (MAD) and "mad" indeed it is, today. This doctrine is based on the twin notions that (1) No defense is possible against nuclear weapons carried by missiles and, (2) No rational nation will strike another if the victim can strike back strongly enough to assure annihilation of the aggressor.

This doctrine was, in fact, technically and philosophically correct *at the time* (mid-1950's) of its adoption as the basis for our national defense development policies. Then, neither we nor anyone else knew how to defend against nuclear-bomb-carrying ICBM's. In the Soviet Union at about that time another very different doctrine was emerging. This formed its roots in the rightly-placed Soviet faith in the power of technical development to lead to new capabilities and thus to *new allowable ground rules.*

In 1957 the great Russian physicist, Peter Kapitza—then a principal scientific advisor to Khrushchev—wrote his convictions that defense against nuclear weapons was, in principle, feasible and inevitable but that it would require the development of "great energetics." He foresaw the need for the development of massive defensive-weapons systems of very large power and very large scale, but saw no basic technical obstacles to their development. Significantly, in the same journal in 1957 in which Kapitza published his article with these views, the next paper was by Bertrand Russell, that peculiarly misguided pacifist, who asserted that, "the way to avoid nuclear war is to ban nuclear weapons." This odd view finds its current public fantasy in the so-called "nuclear freeze" movement. So we have the viewpoints of East vs. West in 1957; Kapitza in Russia outlining technology to avoid nuclear killing by the development of defensive weapons; Russell in England urging negotiation to avoid such development.

Inside the Soviet Union the policy followed was Kapitza's, and by 1960 a new Soviet doctrine emerged and became the basis for all Soviet policy to the present day. This doctrine said that, "there *is* going to be a nuclear war, and we (the Soviet Union) are going to develop the tools to win it." Outside the Soviet Union their policy was to agree with Russell, and they embarked with us on a long series of treaty negotiations designed to weaken us, to limit nuclear weapons testing in the atmosphere, to limit testing underground (which they have broken several times), to ban weapons from space, to limit ABM systems and developments, to stop, limit, restrict—in any way possible—the development of the very technologies and weapons systems needed for Kapitza's defense against nuclear attack, which they themselves were following with great national efforts.

So our politicians and our media opinion-makers bought the idea of negotiation and the lack of Soviet threat, and have been selling it to us (and themselves) ever since. And this is why we find ourselves embroiled in negotiations and debates over arms limitations and policies of co-existence and accommodation—it is a result of twenty years of Soviet nibbling at our will by constant reinforcement of the Russell doctrine in the West, supported by our own tendencies toward peace and our own initial belief in the MAD doctrine, carried forward to the present day. It is like unto King George III and the twenty years of gradual oppression of free citizens of the Colonies which so troubled our Founding Fathers.

But, like those times, the truth of the world situation has long since changed over our twenty year span of time. The MAD doctrine, once true, has become less and less so with the passage of time and

with the continuing advance of science and technology,
until today it is incontrovertibly false and is "mad"
indeed. To pretend to believe in its original precepts
in the face of Soviet and our own technical advances
since Kapitza is as mad as the "MAD" doctrine
itself.

Part of our willingness to cling to this doctrine is
our general American belief that, "the best defense is
a good offense." But, like all other cliches, this one is
true sometimes and false others. Just ask the Washington Redskins if their "DE-FENSE" was crucial in
winning ball games in past years. Or, for those of us
old enough to remember, it was the technology-based
defense of radar target acquisition which enabled
the British to defeat Hitler's Luftwaffe in the Battle
of Britain. There a handful of RAF planes and pilots
slaughtered the best of the German air force on their
nightly raids over England, and made the price so
high that Hitler abandoned plans for a cross-channel
invasion and instead turned east into the impassable
morass of ground war in the Soviet Union. On the
other side lies the example of the German defeat of
France, where the offensive power of the Luftwaffe
overflew the "impregnable" Maginot Line of France.
Here the fault lay in building a defensive system—
the Maginot Line—which had absolutely no capability against the **real** threat, the Nazi air force.

Offense and defense are both necessary, whether in
football, business, or strategic conflict. Our fault over
the past twenty years of MAD doctrine has been to
fail to recognize the erosion of our ability to defend
America *by offense alone,* to ignore the Soviet buildup
of defensive capability to our offense, and to be lulled
(with help from the Russian propaganda mills and
our own media) into a belief that—somehow—the
building of an American defense against the ugly and
ever more powerful Soviet offense would be warlike
and destabilizing of world peace.

*   *   *

We Can Have A Real Defense

The only known way to defend against nuclear missile attack is to destroy the missiles or their nuclear weapon payloads before they reach their targets. But, can this be done? The answer, based on all modern technology, is a resounding YES; and this answer comes in several stages in time and over several stages in the flight of the attacking missile system.

Today the only way we know absolutely how to destroy missiles and warheads is to blow them up. This can be done by intercepting them with fast rocket interceptors carrying non-nuclear or nuclear explosive warheads. The use of nuclear explosive warheads for defense against missiles in the atmosphere can cause problems for the defenders, by radar blackout, fallout from one's own defensive bombs, etc. Thus, non-nuclear defense from the target area of ground targets is best done with normal explosives. In space, however, nuclear weapons do not create such problems for the residents of Earth, and their use there is quite effective and sensible. Even so, it is possible to intercept ICBMs from space platforms *without* use of nuclear weapons, again by using fast rocket interceptors carrying non-nuclear warheads. The most important feature of such non-nuclear defensive systems is that *they can be built now,* for they do *not* require any new technology or science for their construction. All that is needed is our national will to pay the cost of such systems for our own survival.

Beyond these early and buildable non-nuclear defensive systems lie the exotic defenses of the "star wars" era; defensive weapons which shoot beams of light, or atomic particles at light speeds—the so-called "directed energy weapons"—and still others which use nuclear bombs themselves to drive the directed energy of x-rays. Development of the technology of these is underway, but in need of vastly more effort for success in time to yield effective systems based on them, to replace the non-nuclear defensive systems we can build now by new installations around the turn of the century. Today, we now see as possible a full panoply of means to ring our territory with nation-saving defenses against any attack, capable of improvement over the years as new and more advanced technologies are proven practical. If we are to succeed in saving America *we can and must start now* with what we now know how to do. To fail to do so would be to abandon our original commitment to the cause of liberty and free men, and thus to fail not only ourselves but to allow the death of the last bright hopes of our troubled world.

Towards A New Beginning

The size and scale of defensive systems using non-nuclear warheads to shoot at enemy missiles is much greater than that of similar systems using nuclear warheads. So what? All this means is that we must build and deploy a great many of these hypervelocity rocket "shotgun" systems to ensure the safety of our own defended sites and cities. But that is exactly what we Americans do best—develop what we know how to develop, and manufacture it with precision and in quantity. Installing such systems around the country where defense is most needed from the ground will provide a straightforward means of reducing the Soviet's current ability to take out our MAD-based retaliatory strike force, and can be used to defend our cities as well. Because this non-nuclear method is not as powerful as nuclear weapons, it can only provide a partial defense, but in this case *some* defense is better than none.

The next step in achieving a new American independence of action is the development, manufacture and deployment in space—in earth orbit—of similar high-speed non-nuclear "shotgun" systems. Studies of the value of these for destruction of enemy missiles after launch show that some 400 to 500 of these space defense stations will be enough to provide a sensible degree of defense. No defensive system is or ever will be perfect; what is needed is one that makes the enemy lose too much to make an attack worthwhile. Here, as for ground defense, we *know* exactly how to go about this, no new science or technology is involved, only new systems. And American industry could be put to work tomorrow to start the building of these new and better guns over our fireplaces.

The cost of such a space "umbrella" and ground "screen" is enormous, but it is far, far less than the value of New York, or Washington, Chicago, Atlanta, New Orleans, Philadelphia, Denver, Dallas, Houston, Seattle, Portland, Salt Lake City, San Francisco or Los Angeles—or of the rest of the country—or of all of our people who live in these places and in the American countryside. In fact, the cost of both ground and space "shotgun" systems, fully deployed, is considerably *less* than we have spent over the past twenty-five years on the "Triad" (SAC, ICBM, SLBM forces) of offensive systems required by the MAD doctrine for retaliatory delivery of nuclear bombs on an enemy who had already attacked us and laid our land in waste. It is conservatively estimated that the real cost (in today's dollars) of that past expenditure is over $200 billion dollars. The simplest, easiest, most straightforward American "shotgun" systems fully deployed in ground and space defense systems would cost less than one-third of this. **Full** deployment would take about twelve years; about the time required to make a Nation from our Independence start in 1776. Certainly safe defense is worth at least a third as much as post-destruction offense.

But, that is not all. Starting down this road can and will give America a new breath and smell of free air on a new and grander frontier than ever confronted us in the Great Western Wilderness on this continent. This new frontier is the High Frontier of space. We have *sampled* this in the Apollo program when our Flag went on the Moon, and we continue now with our Shuttles as they climb American-orbit-

216 Jerry Pournelle and Dean Ing

bound from the Cape. But a real national expansion into space will be a natural result of securing the high ground out there for the defense of our homes, our cities and our defending military bases—our cavalry forts in the Wilderness of the High Frontier. Imagine 500 American defensive stations in orbit, each carrying a crew of 6 to 8 Americans dedicated to the defense of our free Republic. Three or four thousand of our people in orbital peace-keeping duty; not far removed in concept from the old U.S. Army forts in the Western Wilderness frontier lands of the 1850's. And, like them, the precursor of the nation's expansion into this new territory, for peaceful development of space industry, solar power, and eventually of U.S. colonies in space and on the Moon and other planets of the solar system. New homes for our people, new industries, new and productive jobs in the millions, new hopes for our children and for theirs, new worlds for the expansion of the ongoing American Dream of freedom, and the final suppression of the international political disease of State collectivism which, in our recent and current times, threatens to extinguish the fires of freedom of the Western world.

What better way to ensure our survival than to do so with the means we know best, while building a future for the expansion of American enterprise; continuing and expanding the dream of freedom to work and live in peace and be oneself, at peace with the world and with one's own God. *Now* is the time to act, to start down this new long and murky road to a renewal of our nation's Founder's vows, hopes, and dreams. Like them we can not know how it will all come out. But, like them we must have the courage to begin, secure in the faith that the precepts of liberty will triumph again, and again, *if only we have the will and the energy to make the future happen.* To fail now, to let freedom die a slow and quiet shameful death under the ever-growing might of oppressive foreign tyrants, can lead only to the darkness of a thousand-year night upon the land. *Let us now make a new Declaration of Independence* for our times and our conditions, and take pride in the tasks and responsibilities this will require of us to lead America into a new and glorious future. Let us now, once again, honor our Constitutional imperative to "provide for the Common defense" of our still new nation in its grand experiment of individual liberty and justice for all.

Wargaming:
Time Factors In ICBM Defense

Stefan T. Possony
1 August 1983

Let us assume both Red and Blue have ICBM forces in about equal strength and with comparable readiness. Assume Red attacks Blue's missile sites, with the expectation that he will achieve a 95% kill. Blue sits out the attack, and is left with 5% of his original strength. Red would have disarmed himself, and Blue's remnant would be the only ICBM force which is left in the game.

Blue would have been hit by Red's full force (minus the standard deductions), while Red would not have suffered any damage. Yet depending on various numbers, reliability, targets, and demographic and industrial damage, Blue would possess a real military capability of emerging as victor. Accordingly, if Red attacked because he wished to prevail, he should have known that he needed numerical superiority and a ready reserve. Blue survived because during the pre-war period he negated Red's threat through simply preserving numerical balance.

Assume now that Red achieved a slight numerical superiority, and that Blue deployed a space-based warning and command system. This allows Blue to launch as soon as Red launched, and before Red's missiles impact on Blue's silos. Thus, both sides "unload" on each other. The outcome would tend to be this: no victor, and two losers. If persuasively predicted, this outcome would presumably strengthen deterrence. However, if for technical or political reasons, Blue does not exercise the launch-under-attack option, he probably will suffer a serious setback or defeat.

Suppose Red is dissatisfied with being deterred, and decides Blue's warning-command system must be neutralized or eliminated before a strike against terrestrial targets is risked. This would mean that war must be initiated some time before Red launches his ICBMs. The pre-strike war would result in a nuclear exchange, perhaps of a chaotic type. Red, who diverted much strength to the attack on targets in space, may have reduced his missile strength, and Blue's strength may have declined because he lost a portion of his space sensors. However, Blue may have struck in strength as soon as Red began his attack in space.

In other words, the mere existence of a warning system—which serves only the defender, while the attacker needs an assessment capability during the first phase—has inserted a cushion **before** the attacker is able to impact. This change is effective **regardless** of whether the defender acts on the warning or not.

The futuristic counter to this situation is a ground-based beam weapon which can neutralize the space sensors with complete surprise and at relativistic speed. For so long as no counter is in being, the beam attack could precede the missile strike by a few minutes or less. Such a turn would tend to restore the dominance of the offensive.

Now let us look at timing factors if Blue deploys anti-ICBM defenses.

1. High Frontier satellites carrying and firing anti-ICBM weapons. Since a substantial number of satellites would be needed and satellites cannot be instantly positioned, such a system must be deployed long before Red's ICBMs are launched. Red may counter-deploy a similar satellite system, in order to use it prior to his missile attack. The reduction and elimination of the Blue system, presumably, would take considerable time. So the old problem would be recreated: by striking at the satellites, Red would give advance warning that he is getting ready to launch his missiles, and Blue would know that a missile attack by Red is impending. As soon as Blue loses one satellite to enemy action, he would be legally entitled to pre-empt the enemy's first strike force.

a. A space attack from the ground with missiles would run into exactly the same problem: suppose ASATs were available in adequate numbers, i.e., they would equal the target numbers in the High Frontier system and include supplements to compensate for misses. However, the target system is spread around the globe and cannot be taken down by a volley. The attack could be completed during one revolution, or faster if Red's ASATs were so positioned that they are able to engage several Blue satellites per time unit. But in the absence of a volley, Blue receives excellent warning.

b. Is there a solution for Red? Yes, theoretically he could deploy a satellite system in such a way that *at any moment* one Red satellite could aim at one High Frontier satellite. This would be an elegant solution, but perhaps a difficult one to implement. Repositioning of the High Frontier assets would be an obvious initial counter, but it is premature to discuss this problem now.

2. EMP. Suppose Blue's warning and defense system were supplemented by a force of ICBMs carrying EMP warheads; the pulses can be directed and the swarm of attacking ICBMs be covered with sufficient intensities. If the EMP missiles were started as soon

as the enemy launch is confirmed, they could rise at $D+10$ minutes. Flight time to the area where the boost phase is executed would take a minimum of 20 minutes. Hence the EMP would be ready at $D+30$ minutes, but by that time Red's attacking ICBM arrived at their targets. Thus EMPs could not interfere with the boost of Red missiles. However, the Blue EMP-ICBMs can cover the third or terminal phase of the attack. This may not be desirable because the pulse might affect Blue's territory. Nevertheless, as a defense *in extremis,* EM pulses against warheads, which approach their targets and whose course may be subject to correction, such an operation would be effective. The time requirements of the EMP launch, if only the enemy's terminal phase is to be affected, are relaxed, comparatively speaking.

3. Pop-up of beam weapon. Assume that the beam has a 10,000-kilometer range and moves with relativistic speed. The weapon would be lifted upon receipt of warning and would have to be positioned in substantial altitude. The pop-up probably cannot be initiated before $D+10$ minutes and be completed before $D+15$. That is, in the pop-up mode the beam cannot interfere with the enemy's boost phase. But it could cover much of the mid-phase and all of the terminal phase. Since this is not entirely satisfactory, the question arises whether a really modern and streamlined C^3+I system would not permit pop-up within less than five minutes, with initiation of the actual beam operation upon command after the hostile attack is confirmed. Otherwise, the pop-up solution may be "timely" against ICBMs, but it would probably not be fully effective against SLBMs.

4. Beam weapons on orbit. This solution would obviously ease the timing problem.

a. The orbital weapons could be attacked—slowly—from the ground by missiles. However, the beam weapon should have self-defense capabilities, or be deployed together with an "anti-ASATs" capability. The beams also should be capable of intercepting a large number of ASATs.

b. Blue's orbital beam weapon could be attacked by a beam weapon. If Red's beam weapon has inadequate range, it must be lifted, and the lifting body, e.g. a missile, could be attacked from orbit, as explained under 4a.

c. If both sides have beam weapons with long ranges, Blue's orbital weapon could be attacked by Red from the ground, and it could retaliate against a ground target. It is conceivable that Red's attack can be instituted with complete surprise, and that therefore the orbital weapon would be taken down or neutralized within seconds. This contingency was already mentioned, and would constitute optimal strategic chance.

c(a). It is a mistake to ascribe specific capabilities and operational characteristics to weapons which are as yet unbuilt. The beam weapon, or some beam weapons, may function without concurrently producing indicators, or such a miracle may not be feasible. The orbital beam weapon may work without leaving "tracks," except that, for example, the weapon must be fired by command which must not be secure. The ground beam weapon must heat the atmosphere, and this may result in "tell-tale" signs. And so on.

c(b). It is not possible to tie this complex, which is not yet unfolding, to the operational timing problems of war initiation. Evidently, if beam weapons function on both sides with maximum surprise and, in effect, preclude warning, a most unstable military situation would arise. In addition, if the operations of beam weapons are undetectable, the offensive may recover its dominance, and do so with a vengeance.

c(c). Supposing the beam attack can be discovered, what are the counter-measures? At present, none have become known. But, in line with historical patterns, perhaps beams can be used against beams. This entire complex is not yet relevant, and unless solid information is forthcoming soon, it should not influence decisions which apply to the current period.

d. Nevertheless, even if orbital basing of beam

weapons is technologically not yet risky, and may not be inadvisable at the time when the first weapons of this type are becoming available, a successor basing system actually seems to be in the making, and could be considered as optimal. The alternative to orbital basing necessarily would involve orbital and altitudinal mobility and flexibility, and a capability of evading attack and of overwhelming systems which are tied to fixed orbits. Such a system could develop from the progression of Shuttle technology and the design of spaceplanes, as well as the combination of the two systems.

Strategic Dynamics
And
Space-Laser weaponry

by

Maxwell W. Hunter, II

31 October 1977

[Editor's note:
Carried by the notorious Laser "Gang of Four" to Washington for briefings to Congress and the Pentagon, this is the infamous "Halloween Paper" which helped to spark early interest in space-based ballistic missile defenses. It is included in this report not only for its historic value, but because it is still the best description of defensive strategy for space-based ballistic missile defenses.]

Lockheed Missiles & Space Company, Inc.
Sunnyvale, California

INTRODUCTION

The subject of this dissertation is the current strategic posture of the human race on this planet. This posture consists of a Balance of Terror, a very apt name, in which either of the major sides are presumed capable of devastating the other in a very short period of time. This is the end product of the monstrous energy releases made possible by the nuclear developments started in World War II combined with the extremely short flight time of ballistic missiles so that effective defense has been widely construed to be impossible. Although no one with any sense of history wants to be accused of using the words "Ultimate Weapon," the United States actually has decided that ballistic missiles with thermonuclear warheads are the Ultimate Weapon. We assume everyone else believes this implicity and that, therefore, The Weapon will never be unleashed. Our world is one of Mutual Assured Destruction and our strategic posture is to take all possible steps to ensure that it so remains including ensuring that we are, and are known to be, defenseless. The United

States has embraced a static strategy and rejected all thoughts that strategy is, by its nature, dynamic.

The basis of this discussion is that time and technology advance implacably. High energy lasers are proliferating, and space transportation is about to become sufficiently economical that, if it is used to place such lasers in space, an effective defense against even massive ballistic missile exchanges (and other strategic weapon exchanges such as high altitude bombers), is, indeed, possible. This defense, in addition, would utilize no weapons of mass destruction. Instead, a small but very adequate amount of energy would be placed very precisely at great ranges upon the necessarily flimsy flight vehicles which deliver the weapons of mass destruction. This is the only new strategic concept to present itself in a number of decades, and the only one which merits the words . . . potentially decisive. It should be implemented with all due haste.

The first realization on the author's part that lasers combined with good space transportation would yield a spectacular new strategic option came in January 1967. Although some introductory philosophical material has been prepared in piecemeal in the intervening decade, this is the first attempt to create a somewhat comprehensive discussion of the resulting strategic options in simplified form. The appendix contains six simple mathematical relationships pertinent to the use of space laser weaponry. It is included in an attempt to show the fundamental simplicity of the basic reasoning, but it is not required reading. The paper does not necessarily represent the views of any agency or company which may have conducted studies in this area. It is the viewpoint of the author. It urges that it is now time to counter the Balance of Terror with Precision Space Weaponry and maintains that the sooner we do this, the sooner we can all be freed from the MAD posture.

EVOLUTION OF THE MAD POSTURE

Periodically there have been basic changes in the manner of conducting warfare. Most recent of these, of course, was the development of nuclear weaponry. The overwhelming energy release per pound of material obtainable from nuclear reactions has created almost a religious feeling that it will be impossible to have a major strategic battle in the future since there is, for fundamental reasons, no way of fighting nuclear weapons except a massive exchange with more of the same. This, we are told, would destroy the human race and is thus unthinkable. It was labeled memorably by Churchill ... "The Balance of Terror." This type of perspective—the Ultimate Weapon Syndrome—has, of course, arisen relentlessly throughout history. The synergistic effect of combining the nuclear weapon energy release with the rapid means of delivery made possible by ballistic missiles compounded this syndrome. In the eyes of realistic humans, it seemed impossible to make the necessary national decisions with the degree of contemplation appropriate for such momentous events during the 30 minute flight time of an ICBM.

A nuclear weapon is a means of producing large amounts of destructive energy—on the order of 20 million times for a given weight of material more than that possible with any chemical energy release. This extremely efficient energy package has had such a profound impact on the logistics of delivery to target that comparatively small ballistic missile or airplane fleets can now destroy even a large nation, and perhaps the surface of the entire planet. This monstrous energy release is, of course, uncontainable and spreads essentially isotropically in all directions at once from the point of detonation. Any defense would have to stop essentially all intruders, for if even relatively few bombs get through, the results are devastating. This caused many people decades ago to question if even a defense against aircraft was feasible.

The intercontinental ballistic missile, with its small size, extreme speed (10 times faster than a supersonic bomber) and consequently short flight time (30 minutes), when combined with nuclear warheads, put defense planners into cultural shock. It was at first widely believed that ballistic missiles were impossible to intercept ("You can't hit a needle with a needle!"). That proved false. But the ICBM generates all of its speed at the start of its flight close to home, then shuts down its engines and coasts through space guided unerringly by Newton's Laws with speed undiminished except for gravitational changes. If it deploys decoys, chaff, balloons, or other confusion devices after engine shut-down, they obey the same laws of physics and will remain in formation with the warheads automatically until atmospheric entry at the target. It is, furthermore, difficult if not impossible to be sure one has killed an incoming warhead (short of total vaporization) for warheads, too, continue on the same trajectory even when dead. It seemed that huge numbers of interceptor missiles would be required to stop the results of one ICBM launch, and that the consequent expense for a total defense was not affordable, even by the USA.

To fight against a ballistic missile fleet became "to fight the impossible battle." The total thought process of our land became "There's no defense like a good offense." It became dogma that there was no way to stop ballistic missiles after their launch. Fear of retaliation, however, might well prevent their launch. We built and deployed a large and effective ballistic missile fleet which was, for some time, markedly superior to that of the USSR. After this technological achievement, however, for some reason we turned to psychology rather than physics, diplomacy rather than engineering, to protect the greatest technological power on the planet. Our policy abruptly changed from one of satisfying ourselves of our ability to retaliate effectively to one of deliberately helping all enemies to attain that same ability against us. This is called Mutual Assumed Destruction, the MAD posture. One can only guess what the founding fathers might have called it.

Obviously, both parties must work at MADness. Each offense must be overwhelming, or the defense which opposes it must be deliberately emasculated. Both populations are to be held hostage to the balance of terror. Even civil defense, the simple right to attempt to save oneself and family in a disaster, must be suppressed. The reason given for this, incidentally, is that if you even attempt to save your family in the event of war, you are clearly transmitting an aggressive intent to the enemy, for you must be about to start the war. This reasoning is grotesque.

MADness was born in the technological age when no effective defensive could be envisioned in this country against a ballistic missile fleet. Although the work of desperate minds, it was not totally irrational under those circumstances. It is terribly important that both sides play this game according to the rules, however, and that neither side miscalculates that other's intent. It can only work as a continuing policy if all parties freeze in that technological age. All! Once any one abandons making use of the inevitable advance of technology, then it becomes absolutely vital that he do everything possible to stop any such advance, or else his assumptions will crumble. Should any nation delude itself that technology is frozen if that is not really true, that nation will surely place itself in grave danger.

SPACE . . . NEW ARENA FOR WARFARE

Ideally, it would be nice to not fight. Realistically, the human race has not evolved even close to that wishful goal. If one must fight, it would be desirable to fight decisive strategic battles in an arena where no human lived. Space is that arena ... one where an advanced strategic arsenal can be detonated in its entirety with no direct damage to the earth or its peoples. The nuclear energy release of the Sun is equivalent to 500 million 100-megaton bombs per second (1,000,000 times the total earth nuclear stock-pile per second), yet the Sun is the source of all life on earth, not its executioner.

Ideally, then, it would be desirable to force all hostile activities as far into space as possible. The notion that the human race is forever doomed to exist like two scorpions in a bottle is unimaginative pre-space-age thinking, to say the least. To maintain space as a sanctuary from war, thereby insuring that if the weapons are unleashed they will all detonate where the humans live, is a cruel, genocidal hoax. But war can be attracted to the space environment only if the space forces must be confronted in space to ensure victory. To force hostilities into space, the space forces must be capable of dominating or at least strongly upsetting the opposing earth-bound strategic force balance.

Following Sputnik, considerable study and conjecturing centered on the use of space for military purposes. Some of the early studies recognized that a massive retaliatory force could be deployed in space; however, this was not economically sensible at the time when compared to the use of conventional retaliatory forces. There were some studies in the 1960's on the use of a space force for defense against ballistic missiles by launching rockets from satellites to intercept the missiles early in their flight while the engines were still burning (boost-phase intercept). The utilization of rocket interceptors deployed from moving space stations, however, demands vast quantities of interceptors for effective defense coverage. The systems were unfeasible economically and marginal from a technology standpoint. The space forces envisioned at that time could not affect the strategic balance of the terrestrial forces. They would simply have made the Balance of Terror more expensive.

In spite of these dubious results, space was considered by many military philosophers ... who reasoned by historical analogy ... to be a natural extension of the military arena, just as the sea and air evolved as operational arenas in past ages. This implied the deployment of weapons in space for use both in space and against terrestrial forces, as well as its use for gathering and transmitting information. The early weapon studies were terminated quickly, and subsequent efforts were limited only to those support activities which were useful to the terrestrial weapon forces, a situation exactly analogous to the first decade of military aircraft usage when all U.S. Army airplanes were owned by the Signal Corps. The prohibitive cost of space transportation was the underlying fundamental reason given for this action.

With the emergence of the Space Shuttle and its potential for greatly reducing space transportation costs, the previous studies based on conventional rocketry become due for extensive re-evaluation. When space transportation attains sizable economies, then space weaponry must be evaluated on the basis of military utility rather than being summarily dismissed because of presumed huge logistics costs. Such weaponry need not be placed in primitive, flimsy satellites. Rather, heavy weights of shielding and hardening material (armor, if you will) become feasible in space. The term "battle station" is more descriptive of these weapons than the images conjured up by the terms satellite or space station.

Space forces, furthermore, appear to have basic characteristics which are especially suited to the nature and evolving posture of the United States. We are the strongest nation on earth technically and economically but are having increasing diplomatic and even economic problems with the maintenance of overseas forces and base structures. A space force which blankets the planet requires no overseas bases, a situation quite different from Pax Brittanica. It is a high technology item, and likely expensive, but the money is all spent at home stimulating our own economy. It can only, at the present time, be developed and deployed by large, modern countries. We should be searching for just such weapon systems, be eager to deploy them and have available the many strategic and diplomatic options they yield which are currently not available to us. Strategic dynamics can be extremely beneficial to a technologically vital nation.

DIRECTED ENERGY . . . NEW INTERCEPT TECHNIQUE

High energy lasers which deliver destructive energy at the velocity of light offer a fundamentally different way of performing the functions of interception and have overwhelming advantages over conventional interception technology. The velocity of light is 50,000 times faster than rocket interceptors can achieve. Rocket interceptors, in addition, lose valuable time accelerating, and time is all-important in the deadly business of interception. It is also possible to generate directed energy beams using electrons or larger particles. Particle beams will not move at the velocity of light but may achieve a large fraction of it. Only lasers will be discussed here, for they appear to me to be by far the most effective. If other directed energy beams should be even more effective, the conclusions are even stronger.

When one is destroying cities, the undirected energy release of nuclear bombs is reasonably efficient, since about half of the energy will be deposited in the target area. If, on the other hand, one is only trying to destroy a small target such as a ballistic missile or airplane in flight, the release of extreme energies, most of which miss the target, is merely inefficient and expensive. Lasers are able to project energy in extremely narrow beams. The precision of such beams is so fine that they can exceed the ability of nuclear weapons to concentrate destructive energy in a small area at a distance. In fact, they excel by a factor of one million, and in addition, can concentrate the energy into short time pulses which also exceed nuclear weapon time concentrations by another factor of one million. This fundamental trade seems to escape most people probably because of the overwhelming syndrome that nothing could be more destructive for any purpose than a nuclear bomb.

The ability to concentrate beams of energy moving at the velocity of light so narrowly that they overwhelmingly exceed nuclear bomb energy density delivery capability should be recognized as a weapons achievement with implications every bit as shattering as the development of the monstrous but uncontrolled energy release of the nuclear bombs themselves. This is interception par excellence.

Everyone is familiar with the terrible decision process presented by the ballistic missile forces. If some are unleashed, deliberately or accidentally, only a 30-minute period is available to decide the magnitude of the attack, and whether a full scale World War III will be initiated in response. Any weapon system which would permit more time in the human decision process will, by definition, have to stop any initial attack automatically. In particular, it would be necessary for the system to go to war within less than a minute in order to prevent saturation of the system by the magnitude of a large attack. Reasonable amounts of time for human decision-making can only be realized by having a balance-of-terror negating system which goes to war almost instantaneously. Since automatic equipment, like humans, should not be expected to be perfect, the system, then, must not be capable of evoking the response of a World War III onslaught in the event of system mistakes. It follows that the system must not be capable of mass destruction in any possible accidental situation, or the cure will be identical to the disease.

The high directivity characteristics of lasers are vital to solving this decision dilemma. Lasers represent an extremely precise control of rather small total amounts of energy. A 25 megawatt laser, as an example, if focused on a ballistic missile, deposits on the surface of that missile in a 5-second period the energy equivalent of about 50 lbs. of high explosives. Thus adequate energy packages are readily delivered to ensure the destruction of flight weight vehicles . . . after all, only a few pounds of high explosives are required to stop a ballistic missile if the explosive can just be placed on the missile. The laser thus does not employ monstrous nuclear energy releases and hence is not a weapon of mass destruction but rather one of discrete destruction. The fact that lasers cannot be weapons of mass destruction is crucial for the human decision process.

LASERS FROM SPACE . . . THE NEW SYNERGISM

A new synergism, the advent of high energy lasers coupled with their installation in space, can cause profound changes in the MAD posture. When lasers are placed in space so that every location on this planet is placed continuously in the target area of a laser battle system, then one has a right to expect truly fundamental changes. It raises the distinct possibility that the rapid delivery of nuclear explosives can be prevented by a weapon system which is itself not capable of mass destruction. Such a system would clearly give the nation that possesses it options in strategic posture and activitiy which are now denied everyone, including returning to the human beings in charge the time to permit adequate decision making which was taken from them by the unholy synergism of nuclear weaponry and ballistic missiles.

Interception of enemy ballistic missiles during their boost phase is likely the most efficient means of combatting strategic missiles. During boost, the number of targets is minimum and their vulnerability is maximum. The missiles have maximum internal pressure and the tank walls are at maximum temperature so that minimum energy is required to destroy the vehicle. The missiles also must generate massive exhaust plumes which decidedly enhances detection. The destruction of one missile, furthermore, negates all of its MIRVs. If an enemy has been upgrading his offense by increasing the number of MIRVs per launch vehicle, he has wasted his resources when the missiles are destroyed during boost. Furthermore, sea-based missiles are as easily negated by boost-phase intercept as land-based missiles, and the coverage of the sea-based launches is obtained at zero cost when a space-based system is used.

Kills during boost phase can be reliably and accurately assessed by simply measuring the missiles' velocity change. This represents a tremendous operational advantage. Once the missile has stopped generating velocity, its impact area is precisely known. If it is destroyed prior to its intended cut-off velocity, the debris and warhead . . . dead or alive . . . will land short of the target area, often in the oceans and frequently, with poetic justice, in the homeland of the launching country. After burnout, however, the re-entry hardened targets become cold bodies and apparently multiply in number by large factors through deployment of their threat tubes of chaff, decoys, etc. Everything lands in the target area. Decoying changes from difficult before velocity cut-off to relatively easy afterward since afterward almost no energy is required to keep the threat tube properly positioned with respect to the warheads.

Ballistic missiles can be stopped with relatively small amounts of energy. They always will be, since they must have light structures to move so fast. This must also be true of airplanes or anything else that moves fast. The total energy supplies which must be put in orbit for strategic negation are, although large, well within shuttle logistics capability. There is, however, an even vaster implication to lasers in space than merely ballistic missile defense.

If optical wavelength lasers are used to penetrate the atmosphere, then it is easily conceivable that such weapons can be used for tactical applications. They would be clear-weather weapons, and targeting would be more complex than in the ballistic missile case. Tactical wars, on the other hand, are rarely over in a short period of time. If one could deny clear-weather operations to an enemy, he would have almost overwhelming tactical advantages. The number of tactical targets—airplanes, helicopters, trucks, etc.—vastly exceeds the number of strategic targets—the very limited ballistic missile and bomber forces. In the tactical case, hence, substantially greater power supplies would be required to drive the lasers.

Even though the total energy is much greater, it is impossible for this system to become a weapon of mass destruction. In order to handle the energy—to live with it—so that it can be beamed this precisely, the rate of energy production must be limited to relatively normal values. The monstrous instantaneous energy release of thermonuclear bombs cannot be used. Such a system would work like a ballistic missile defense system—by its ability to precisely pin-point relatively small packages of energy anywhere on or near the planet that it chooses—but, given sufficient time, it could do this for a much greater number of targets.

NUMBERS IN SPACE

It seems intuitively obvious that any space-based defense system would involve astronomical numbers of battle stations in orbit. Clearly, the numbers involved are related to the range of the weapons they carry. The maximum area on Earth will be covered by a weapon with a given range if the weapon maximum effective range is identical to the range to the visible horizon, or Earth's limb in astronomical parlance. Although a laser of 1000 km range will cover only 1/165 of the Earth's surface, a laser with 5000 km range will cover 1/9 of the Earth's surface, and 10,000 km will cover almost ¼ of the Earth's surface.

This does not yet tell the complete story, however, for once again Newton's Laws enter the discussion. Satellites remain in orbit because they have sufficient velocity that their centrifugal force as they circle the Earth counter-balances gravity. Obviously, then, they are moving at great speeds (or else we would have built them centuries ago); and the geometry of their circling orbits must be accounted for in determining the total number of battle stations required for a complete defense.

Assuming polar orbits, the number of battle stations will be 406 if the weapon range is 1,000 km, but becomes only 21 if the weapon range can be extended to 5,000 km and 9 if the range is 10,000 km. A few dozen satellites are easy to envision, but a few hundred, also, should not shock us. The average Naval vessel is much larger and we consider (rightly so) that 1,000 of them are necessary to our peace of mind. We could doom ourselves forever by simply not realizing the fabulous results of applying some ingenuity to space logistics.

One point is difficult to envision. If we talk of lasers killing ballistic missiles with efficiency at ranges of thousands of kilometers, we talk of energy beams only a few meters in width accurately placed on ballistic missiles of the same dimensions. In other words, the guidance precision must be a bit less than one part in a million. It is difficult to envision . . . and to feel comfortable about. We've been here before, however . . . it was also difficult to envision a needle hitting a needle. The key to removing the oppression of the Balance of Terror from the human race is the ability to generate precision. We should become the World leader in precision, instead of always looking for a larger club, or cringing forever.

THE SOCIO-POLITICAL ENVIRONMENT

The socio-political environment of the past decade has undergone dramatic changes. In the field of defense, change is most notable by the signing of the Outer Space Treaty and the Nuclear Test Ban Treaty as well as the SALT agreements. Any new military thinking must properly consider these entities. The pertinent prohibition of the two treaties is against all military activity on celestial bodies but only against activity involving nuclear explosives or other weapons of mass destruction in space itself. These prohibitions strongly inhibit the types of offensive systems deployable in space. The SALT I agreements allow for the creation of new ABM systems based on different physical principles.

A doctrine which has periodically been suggested as a policy of the United States is to retract to a Fortress America to resolve our various difficulties throughout the world. This, in turn, is frequently referred to in horrifying terms as if it were a Maginot

Line type of thinking, which connotates the epitome of defeatism in strategic thinking, and a retreat to isolationism. With a space-based concept, as indicated here, Fortress America would be neither defeatism nor a retreat to isolation. In the grand strategic sense, the heavily armed space weapon system is capable of interacting strongly with sea, air and land forces throughout the globe, even though all of its bases are only in home territory, in fact, perhaps deep in the zone of the interior. Thus, it is possible to gradually retreat from many of our overseas installations without retreating from our overseas commitments. Admittedly, we have been diplomatically failing to maintain the installations in secure fashion, but we need not withdraw from the human race and become merely an isolated country in our own small corner.

The term should not be Fortress America. This would be Pax Americana, with an effectiveness and flexibility never dreamed of in the centuries of Pax Britannia. Any systems which permit us to do this should be extolled as a major feature of this future American posture and not idly dismissed as some wild dream. They would be, of course, a bureaucratic nightmare because of the impact they would have on our current systems.

Interestingly enough, these suggestions can be expected to draw fire from arms controllers and military advocates alike. The arms controllers have masterminded our drift into the feeling that all weaponry and advanced technology is bad. It is a natural feeling, since we have been continually told that there is no possible defense against weapons of mass destruction and we must cringe in our caves forever before this particular Ultimate Weapon. Many military advocates, in turn, revel in our violent offensive capability, and would be chagrined if their power and budgets were to pass to the defense. Both parties would much rather hold all peoples, young and old, as hostages to the Balance of Terror.

I am suggesting here a valid change in our basic thinking, and I would expect it to be widely rejected by many of the advocates of whichever old school. It seems to me that it is time, perhaps overdue, for a re-assessment of this basic decision. It would be a terrible thing to condemn the human race to live forever in a grotesque world of Mutual Assured Destruction, if in fact, the advance of technology had given us the means to create more human alternatives. The use of precision weaponry should become a major desirable feature of our life.

This is a new strategic option which must be understood. If we were to do it when the opposition did not, it would give us commanding options compared to the current situation. If the enemy were to do it and we did not, it would totally negate our current strategic posture. If we pursue international arms control negotiations and do not understand the options which are presented here, we could easily put ourselves into a disastrous position with respect to the future. We should not blindly follow the lead of arms control thinkers who may well have been from a past nuclear age upon which the sun is finally setting. The potential decisiveness of the system is what makes thorough examination at this point in time very desirable.

It seems to me that diplomatically such a system would be easy for our state department to sell to both friends and enemies around the planet. It takes a while to put it in perspective with respect to our diplomacy of the last 30 years with its perfectly legitimate but nonetheless mind-numbing preoccupation with nuclear bombs. Certainly to those of the old school, it would be difficult to conceive of all the diplomatic advantages of a space laser weapon system. We will, after all, have developed a potentially decisive strategic system that is not a weapon of mass destruction. We will be presenting to friend and enemy alike an American posture which says:

We can exist in this world of terror without resorting to mass destruction.

We have engaged in precision technological activities which will enable us to preserve our own freedom of action and will preserve our own nation.

Yet we will use nothing which will be capable of devastating the world.

We will be able to prevent you, who do rely on old-fashioned devastation concepts, from using them on other people, if we choose.

If we so choose, we will not even hurt you.

It seems to me that once the general flavor of this becomes understood in a diplomatic sense, that it can be by far the most positive diplomatic initiative that anyone has ever undertaken. It should be considered in this positive framework rather than merely as a question of possible instability injected into obsolete concepts. Certainly it is unstable to the obsolete concepts . . . for which we should all give thanks.

ULTIMATE WEAPON THOUGHTS

It is not the intention of this paper to create the impression that directed energy weapons in space are in any respect an Ultimate Weapon. Quite the contrary, it is suggested that entirely too many ultimate weapon syndrome thoughts have badly clouded our strategic thinking for several decades. When it was decided that the thermonuclear ballistic missile was the ultimate weapon, strategic dynamics was ignored. No one in charge believed for a minute that they would ever see massive tonnage placed into space, and the fledgling lasers of puny power in those days were derided as something which only a nut on "death rays" would take seriously. That was, as technology goes, a long time ago, and those thoughts and their thinkers must be recognized as belonging to an admittedly spectacular, but nonetheless obsolete, technical age.

Lasers from space can stop ballistic missiles, and other fast-moving delivery systems also. They can stop a full-scale ballistic missile attack with little damage to the defended area for a reasonable cost. They can fight and win the "impossible battle." Obviously, however, such a space weapon force could be defeated in space by a superior (in numbers or quality) force of like composition. One would have to maintain his space laser force second to none into the future in order to remove the Balance of Terror permanently from his land.

If there is an ultimate weapon, it is the will to make the necessary sacrifices to remain strong combined with the intelligence to become a master of strategic dynamics and to change the composition of one's weaponry as time and technology advance. Space laser weaponry is simply another step on the road which must be traveled if we are to remain free. The only ultimate weapon is to not rest on your laurels.

SUMMARY

The space-based laser deployed in adequate quantities by a space transportation system appears to be the only weapon that can reach a ballistic missile force in time to ensure its destruction. Since the laser weapon would not be capable of mass destruction, it would be possible to give the weapon the option of going to war quickly enough to be effective without risking human annihilation. The system would represent, as soon as deployed, an alternative to the Balance of Terror.

In the longer run, since the laser would give a space force the ability to intervene effectively with the most modern of strategic terrestrial forces, it would supply the fundamental link for attracting strategic war away from the planet. That trend ought to be strongly encouraged by anyone who lives on the planet.

Any system which can so intervene in strategic warfare would obviously have many uses, some of them decisive, in limited tactical warfare, when equipped with larger power supplies.

Future space systems should play the same dominant military role that the airborne forces have recently and the sea forces earlier, but without the need for any overseas base structure. Such systems may well be unusually suited to the strategic and diplomatic posture of this nation in the future.

This appendix contains six simple
basic mathematical relationships
which underlie the use of space
laser anti-ballistic missile systems.

A. The mass-energy equivalence.

$$E = mc^2$$

Where E = energy
               m = mass
               c = velocity of light

Einstein's famous equation nicely explains the Balance of Terror. The high value of the velocity of light is about 300 million meters per second. If mass were completely converted to energy, it would have over

25 billion times the energy release of an equivalent mass of TNT. This would require a matter-antimatter reaction. Nuclear fission reactions typically convert about 0.1 percent of mass to energy and fusion reactions about 0.8 percent. If the proper values are inserted for a nuclear explosive which is a mixture of 50% fission and 50% fusion, the energy release of the nuclear material burned is over 24 million times the energy release of a like mass of TNT.

All the intense nuclear development efforts on this planet can be measured by the ability to build bombs of various sizes and, more importantly, by how close either side can now come, considering efficiency of nuclear burning plus the weight required for containment and triggering mechanisms, to the values given in the limit by Einstein's equation. After a few decades development in any technical field, one normally expects the overall engineering efficiency to approach reasonable values regardless of how low the initial experiments may have been. The limit equation, then, becomes the real boundary of the possibilities. When the limits are very high, great changes in thinking are inevitably forced upon us.

B. The diffraction limit.

$$\alpha = \frac{2\,\lambda}{\pi\,D}$$

Where α = beam angle of spreading, radians
λ = wavelength of radiation
D = diameter of aperture

Just as Einstein's equation governs the monstrous energy release of nuclear explosives, so the diffraction limit equation governs the precision of the projection of beams of electro-magnetic energy. In the mathematically purest sense, this paper discusses mortal combat between these two equations.

As the extremely high value of the velocity of light dominates the mass-energy equivalence, so the extremely small wavelength of light dominates the diffraction limit of lasers. The wavelength of light is less than a millionth of a meter, and the projecting aperture of a laser can be many meters, so that the beam spreading can be less than one part in a million.

The constant $2/\tau$ applies to the case of a circular aperture projecting a beam of perfectly flat wavefront with a Gaussian intensity distribution. In actual lasers, the beam will have neither a perfectly flat wavefront nor a completely Gaussian intensity distribution. The entire spectrum of detailed engineering development of lasers is summarized both by how powerful and what wavelength lasers can be built and by how close one can come to perfect "beam quality." This equation also specifies capabilities that must be achieved by the beam pointing and tracking systems if the lasers are to be used efficiently.

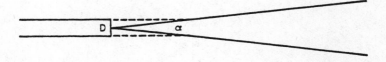

C. The energy concentration ratio.

$$R = \frac{2}{1 - \cos{(\alpha/2)}}$$

$$= \frac{16}{\alpha^2} \quad \text{for small } \alpha$$

Where: $R = \dfrac{\text{surface area of sphere}}{\text{area of beam at sphere surface}}$

α = beam angle of spreading

This relationship is dominated by the beam spreading angle. If the ratio of nuclear to chemical energy per pound of 24×10^6 (assuming 100% nuclear efficiency) is used for R, the required value of α is about one thousandth. As previously stated, α can be on the order of one millionth so that, since α appears as a square, lasers using only chemical energy can generate energy density of a million times greater for equal mass than nuclear bombs. For some types of damage, the rate of energy release, or instantaneous power, is important. Nuclear bombs release their radiation in about a millionth of a second, but lasers can concentrate their energy in pulses of a billionth of a second and even as short as a million-millionth of a second. Thus the energy concentration in time can be a million times greater than that of a nuclear bomb.

It is these fabulous concentrations of energy both in space and time that the Balance of Terrorists did not dream could happen.

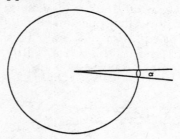

D. Earth coverage of a single beam.

$$F = \frac{1 - \cos \theta}{2}$$

$$= \frac{\theta^2}{4} \quad \text{for small } \theta$$

Where F = fraction of earth surface covered by a single beam

θ = angle at earth center of surface covered by beam

θ is given by:

$$\theta = \arctan \frac{R}{r} \left(\frac{\cos \beta}{1 + \frac{R}{r} \sin \beta} \right)$$

$$= \arctan \frac{R}{r} \quad , \quad \beta = 0$$

Where: R = laser range
          r = earth radius
          β = angle below the horizon that beam is aimed

The maximum possible coverage by a single beam will occur if the maximum range is taken as that to the horizon (or earth's limb). For this case, β = 0. With β = 0, a 1,000 km range laser will cover only 1/165 of the earth, but a 5,000 km laser will cover 1/9 of the earth and a 10,000 km laser will cover almost ¼ of the earth.

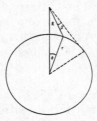

E. Number of battle stations for Earth coverage

$$n \;=\; \frac{\pi}{2\,F}$$

$$=\; \frac{\pi}{1 - \cos\theta}$$

$$=\; \frac{2\,\pi}{\theta^2} \quad \text{for small } \theta$$

Where F and θ are defined as in section D.

n = number of battle stations required for complete earth coverage neglecting orbital velocity.

This is the minimum conceivable number of stations. It accounts for the fact that each battle station covers a circular rather than square area of the Earth's surface and it is hence necessary that they overlap for complete coverage. The overlap factor is π/2. The minimum conceivable number is shown as a function of laser range in the figure on the next page.

We must, of course, account for the gravitationally necessary high-velocity orbits.
Then

$$N = \frac{\pi^2}{2\left(\text{arc cos } \sqrt{\cos \theta'}\right)^2}$$

$$= \frac{\pi^2}{\theta^2} \quad \text{for small } \theta$$

Where   N = number of battle stations required for for complete earth coverage assuming polar orbits.

This number is also shown as a function of laser range in the figure. The difference between the two curves represents the inefficiency of additional overlap due to orbital dynamics. It ranges from $\pi/2$ (63.6 percent efficient) at 1,000 km to 1.30 (76.9 percent efficient) at 10,000 km.

These are surprisingly good efficiencies. There likely are orbital patterns with more efficient coverage than pure polar orbits, but the improvement is limited to some (probably small) portion of these factors.

These expressions assume that fractions of battle stations and orbital rings are possible, which cannot be. Actual deployments with integer numbers of battle stations and rings will closely approximate, and frequently lie exactly on, the curve so that this simple approximation is quite accurate and useful.

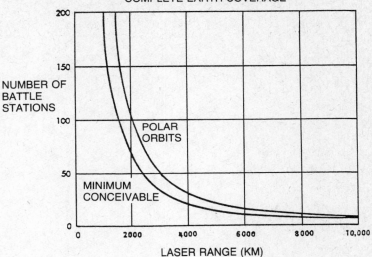

REQUIRED NUMBER OF BATTLE STATIONS
COMPLETE EARTH COVERAGE